Jedidiah Boone

Other Westerns by Dusty Rhodes

Man Hunter

Shiloh

Available at

Sundowners

A Division of

Treble Heart Books

Jedidiah Boone

Treble Heart Books
1284 Overlook Dr.
Sierra Vista, AZ 85635-5512
http://www.trebleheartbooks.com

ISBN: 1-931742-64-2

Jedidiah Boone

Dusty Rhodes

Presented by

SUNDOWNERS
A division of
Treble Heart Books

Chapter One

A shrill scream pierced the early morning stillness and invaded eleven year old Elizabeth Fargo's dream world. She bolted upright to a sitting position in bed and blinked the world into focus. It must have been a bad dream, she tried to reason, swallowing the lump of fear from her throat back down to a churning stomach.

Beside her, Rebecca whined and uncurled herself from the covers, rubbing her sleepy eyes and swiping her long golden hair from her face with the back of a small hand. Something had awoken her, too. Usually, you had to pry her five-year-old sister out of bed.

The ear-shattering blast of a gunshot interrupted her thoughts and exploded the air around them and-then another!

Elizabeth's body jerked with each shot and went cold, as terror spiraled through her. Her ears rang. Rebecca screamed and plunged into her arms, shaking uncontrollably. Elizabeth saw her little sister's eyes go wide in a chalky face, blank with horror, blurry with tears.

Elizabeth encircled her sister with shaky arms and drew her close. They clung to each other, too frightened to cry. Elizabeth's own body quivered and her heart thundered against the wall of her chest. Hot tears breached the rims of her eyes. Her chest contracted and a sob squirmed its way up the back of her throat. They waited-straining, shaking.

"What is it, Liz?" the five year old demanded, her panicky voice quivering.

"I don't..."

The door to their bedroom suddenly burst open, choking off the rest of Elizabeth's words.

Her eyes rounded white. What she saw sent a chill racing up her spine. Standing in the doorway was the first Indian she had ever seen.

Winston Taylor leaned back in the comfortable upholstered chair and drew a long pull on a fat cigar. He inhaled deeply and let the excess smoke slide from his lips in a long, blue tendril that drifted lazily toward the ceiling.

His boss had listened intently as the requested report was given, then, without a word, he had stood and strode to the window. For what seemed an interminable time, William G. Fargo stared out the window, apparently lost in thought.

Winston waited; he knew a lot about waiting. As the youngest of six brothers, it seemed he had spent half of his life waiting for one reason or another: He had waited until his older brothers ate their fill before he was allowed the meager leftovers from the supper table. He waited for their hand-me-down shoes and clothes until they were so worn out they would hardly stay on.

Even at West Point he had waited to be accepted by the snobby sons of the wealthy or high-ranking officers—it had never happened. To their way of thinking, he was just a nobody that shouldn't even have been there and they never missed an opportunity to make that crystal clear. He waited anyway, and watched, and learned. After graduating with honors and receiving his commission as a first lieutenant, he waited some more. Then the Civil War broke out and his waiting was over. He proved himself in battle and rose steadily through the ranks to become a full colonel by war's end. At the age of thirty-eight, after serving twenty years in the military, he retired.

He had gone to work for the Wells Fargo agency shortly after his retirement. Mr. Louis McLane, the president of the agency at the time, hired him and put him in charge of the floundering stagecoach branch of the agency.

It was in trouble and badly in need of new management. In less than six months he had completely turned the business around and expanded it into a nationwide network of more than one hundred eighty stage stations stretched across the country, over twelve hundred head of stock, and employing four hundred men. After buying out the Butterfield stage line, Wells Fargo boasted of delivering passengers from St. Louis to San Francisco in just twenty-five days.

While he waited for Mr. Fargo to finish his thought process, Winston's gaze slowly circled the large, elaborately furnished office. His searching gaze admired the original paintings in gilded frames that hung on wine-colored silk brocade wall covering, and the thick, imported rug on the floor. He noted the wide, mahogany desk with a high-back, leather chair. On the desk were neatly organized stacks of papers and a wooden humidor full of expensive cigars. It was an office befitting the President of the sprawling banking and express conglomerate known as the Wells Fargo Agency.

"How do you know this man…what did you say his name was?" Mr. Fargo finally asked. He didn't bother turning to face his employee. He continued to stare out the window of the red brick building with green trim on Montgomery Street in San Francisco, the headquarters of Wells Fargo.

"Boone," Winston Taylor replied, "his name is Jedidiah Boone. His grandfather was Squire Boone, brother of the famous Daniel Boone, the explorer and frontiersman. Jedidiah served with me in the army as a scout. He's the best I ever saw. They say he can trail a snowflake in a howling blizzard.

"He's worked for us here at Wells Fargo on a couple of special jobs. He's the one who brought in the Wilbourn brothers that robbed so many of our stages up in southern Colorado. He also tracked down and killed Lone Wolf and a half dozen Apaches that ambushed our stage and slaughtered our driver, the shotgun messenger, and eight passengers near El Paso about a year ago."

The big man turned from the window to face Winston. William Fargo was a tall man, big boned with wide shoulders. A leonine shock of salt and pepper hair crowned his head. Both it and his mustache were well trimmed. He wore a dark broadcloth business suit with freshly creased trousers and a starched white shirt. A pearl stickpin gleamed from the cravat cinched around his stiff winged collar. His very appearance conveyed an impression of authority. It seemed his dark, flashing eyes had a way of looking right into a man's soul. Those penetrating eyes were now fixed squarely on Winston Taylor.

"Can this man do what has to be done?" Fargo asked pointedly.

"Mr. Fargo, if it can be done, Jedidiah Boone can do it. The only question is, will he do it?"

"What do you mean?" Winston's boss asked, a concerned furrow plowing across his forehead. "Didn't you say he works for us?"

"Well, no sir, not exactly. Like I say, he's done a couple of jobs for us on occasion, but that was by a special arrangement I made with him. I paid him time, expenses, and the reward we had posted on those fellows. Jedidiah is an independent sort of fellow, always has been. He's his own man, beholden to no one.

"He's mostly a loner. Lives way back in the middle of nowhere, halfway to the sky at a place called Angel Fire Mountain. It's in New Mexico Territory not too far from Taos. He found the place while on a scouting expedition during the war.

"When the fighting was over, he went back to Missouri and

brought back a black man and his wife that had been with the Boone family for years. They built a little log cabin on a shelf about two-thirds up the side of that mountain. Ain't but one way up or down."

"Is he the kind of man we can trust?" Mr. Fargo asked, his probing eyes still fixed on his employee.

"Mr. Fargo, I've trusted Jedidiah Boone with my life on more than one occasion."

"Very well then, it's settled. You and I will go to Sante Fe, New Mexico Territory to meet with this Mr. Boone. We'll take my private coach. I want two of the best drivers we have and two shotgun messengers to ride along. We'll need fresh teams of horses ready and waiting at our stage stations along the way so there will be no delay.

"Arrange a meeting with Mr. Boone in Sante Fe on the thirteenth. I'd like my presence in Sante Fe not be known. As you well know, we're presently involved in delicate negotiations with the government in Washington for the nationwide mail contract. If news of my presence in Sante Fe became public knowledge, it would undoubtedly call attention to the tragic events surrounding my brother and his family.

"Our competitors might somehow use that information to cast doubt on our ability to fulfill the government mail contract. Wells Fargo desperately needs that contract to continue our nationwide expansion.

"Make it appear as if it is you and you alone meeting with Mr. Boone. You will remain in Sante Fe until this matter is resolved. Remember, only you and Mr. Boone are to know of my presence, is that understood?"

"Yes sir," Winston Taylor said briskly and stood to his feet, well aware the meeting was over and he had been excused. "It will be taken care of."

He hurried from the office, cognizant of the importance of his task. Innocent lives and the very future of the Wells Fargo Agency might well depend upon the secrecy and success of this mission.

* * *

A wisp of a cool breeze crept down the high mountain. It whispered through thick stands of golden aspen trees that hugged the steep slopes. Their leaves shimmered like tiny flakes of pure gold and set the mountainside ablaze with splashes of brilliant color.

The morning was half spent and still the tall man sat pushed back in the rocking chair on the front porch of his mountain log cabin. His legs were propped up against a peeled cedar post. Long-fingered hands laced around a steaming cup of coffee. His wheat colored hair hung near shoulder length under an old and battered, dirty-gray Stetson tilted low on his forehead, partly shading his sky-blue eyes. A golden handlebar mustache spread widely above a slash of a mouth. Weather-darkened skin testified to the unmistakable effect of too many days in the sun and belied his twenty-six years.

Behind the cabin, the mountains rose steeply against a backdrop of limitless sky.

Beside him a large wolf dog lay sleeping. As if by some unheard signal the big dog jerked up his head. Narrowly set, dark eyes peered into the distance. A low growl rumbled deep in his huge chest and he climbed to his feet.

"I see 'em," the big man mumbled and swallowed the last gulp of coffee from his cup. He set the cup on the porch, slowly knuckled his mustache, and pulled out the makings for a smoke. Creasing a rolling paper, he sprinkled tobacco into the fold and ran his tongue along the edge. He twirled it, popped a sulfur, and drew a long inhale. His narrowed eyes peered into the distant valley as a slow streamer of blue smoke escaped his lips and drifted upward.

In the valley far below, two riders picked their way laboriously along the bank of the Angel Fire River. A mist rose from the thundering stream and hung in the morning air like a dense fog. The valley clearings were ruffled with flaming dogwoods and lime-green sweet gum trees. Fall violets spread their colorful flowers across the valley floor like a bright blue carpet.

The mountain stream emerged newborn, sparkling fresh and icy-cold, from cavernous rock springs high above and behind Jedidiah's mountain hideaway. It rushed within twenty yards of his log cabin before plunging over the edge of a rock shelf and falling several hundred feet into Angel Fire Valley. It tumbled noisily over and around house-size boulders and fought its way through heavy stands of ponderosa pine as it began its long journey toward the sea. A continuing roar from the valley below drifted up the mountainside.

The riders were still a couple of miles away but even at that distance Jedidiah thought he recognized the black and white pinto. Only one fellow he knew rode a horse like that. He remembered because it looked so much like the brown and white pinto he, himself rode.

"Mose," the big man called out, his deep voice filling the mountain air. "We've got company. Better get the wife inside just in case."

Off to the end of the peeled log cabin, a giant of a man stilled the double-bladed ax from his wood chopping and raised to his full height, a full hand above six feet. Sun glistened off his ebony, sweat stained chest as he lifted a muscled arm to swipe the sweat from his forehead.

"You heard Mr. Boone, woman," his bullfrog voice boomed out.

A heavyset black woman in a flour sack dress and a white apron tied around her ample middle hung the last pair of wet britches across the clothes' line. She scooped up the empty basket and hurried toward the cabin mumbling to herself.

"Lawd amercy," she complained. "How's a body supposed to get her work done around here nohow?"

"Who you reckon it is, Mr. Boone?" the black man asked, arming sweat from his forehead and strolling over to retrieve his own rifle that was canted against the cabin.

"I can't rightly tell for shore," the tall man said, uncoiling himself from the chair, stretching, and leaning a big shoulder against the cedar porch post, the rifle clutched loosely in his left hand. "It seems to me I recall that Wells Fargo detective from down in Santa Fe riding a pinto like that. Don't recognize the other fellow."

They watched the two riders splash across the stream and rein up. The man on the pinto swiped his hat off and mopped the sweat from his forehead with an arm as he raised his gaze to follow the narrow trail up the steep mountainside.

It took another half hour before the riders crested the rocky shelf and walked their horses half a hundred yards across the grassy space toward the mountain cabin.

"Okay if we ride in?" the fellow on the pinto shouted above the roar of Angel Fire Falls.

"Come ahead," Jedidiah replied, lifting the Henry to rest comfortably in the crook of his arm.

The two riders walked their horses slowly forward and pulled up a short distance from the front porch. The rider of the pinto was a tall, thin fellow with shifty eyes and a gaunt looking face. He wore a black broadcloth suit that several days trail dust had turned a dingy brown. A Colt pistol in a cutaway holster rested on his right hip.

The second man was a big, wide-shouldered bear of a man with a barrel chest and a full beard that hid his facial features. He also wore a two-piece suit and one of those funny looking black bowler hats. The bulge under his left coat flap did little to hide the gun in a shoulder holster.

"You'd be Jedidiah Boone, I reckon?" the taller man said, doffing his dusty Stetson and mopping the sweat from the inside sweatband with a red bandanna.

"I'm James Hume. I'm chief of detectives with the Wells Fargo Agency. We've never actually met, but I saw you once over in Taos when you brought in the Wilbourn brothers face down across their saddles. This here is my partner, George Honeycutt."

"I remember you," Jedidiah said. "You were pointed out to me. You fellas just out for a morning ride or did you come with something in mind?" he asked, still not moving his rifle from the crook of his arm. "We don't get many folks up this way."

"Yeah," the one called Hume said. "I can shore see why. A fellow's got to come here on purpose. So this is the mountain they call Angel Fire? We never would have found your place if we hadn't run into a trapper down on the Mora River. We liked to never convinced him into telling us how to find you. He said you didn't take kindly to visitors."

"We ain't much on socializing," Jedidiah said. "Now that you found me, Mr. Hume, what's your business?"

"I come bringing an urgent message for you," the detective said, his voice betraying some displeasure at the task. "Mr. Winston Taylor himself, a vice-president with the Wells Fargo Agency, would like you to meet him in Sante Fe on the thirteenth, that's just three days from now. Don't know if we can make it or not. We've been searching for you for near a week. How far is it from here to Sante Fe?"

"Maybe forty or fifty miles as the crow flies," Jedidiah told them. "But we ain't crows."

"The message said it's urgent," the detective said impatiently. "He's coming all the way from San Francisco by special stagecoach. We're supposed to accompany you there. I figure it's near three days hard ride so we better get started."

"What's he want?" Jedidiah asked.

"The message didn't say, but it must be awfully important. Like I said, Mr. Taylor is coming all the way from San Francisco. I've been with the agency three years and I've never even met him. He's an awfully powerful man though."

Silence stretched on a space. Jedidiah engaged himself in his usual habit of fingering an earlobe while he was in deep contemplation. Finally, having made up his mind, he pushed his shoulder away from the post.

"You boys' lite and sit a spell while I get my things together," Jedidiah told them. "Mose, see if Minnie's got some left over coffee for these fellows. Throw my packsaddle on Mule and saddle my pinto. Load on three days grain ration. I'll gather my trail supplies. You men are welcome to sit the porch. She'll bring some coffee directly."

It took half an hour before Jedidiah toed a stirrup and swung into his saddle. He settled his six foot three frame into the saddle of the brown and white pinto. It had been a spell since the big gelding had limbered his legs and he nervously high-stepped and tossed his head, held in place by a tight rein in a strong hand.

"When you be coming back, Mr. Boone, sir?" the big black man made inquiry.

"Like always, Mose," Jedidiah said. "Look for me when you see me coming."

"That's a fine looking mount you got there," the one called Hume said admiringly. "Just like mine except for the color."

"He'll do," Jedidiah said off-handidly, giving the lead rope to his pack mule a half-hitch around the saddle horn. "Let's go, Dog."

"You mean you're taking that wolf dog with us," Hume asked critically.

"Dog goes where I go," Jedidiah replied, reining the big pinto around and touching his booted heel to a tender flank.

Chapter Two

Just shy of sundown of the third day three trail weary riders plodded down the dusty street of Sante Fe, New Mexico Territory. The Spanish had originally established the town. It lay in an arid, desert valley in the shadow of the Sangre de Cristos. At an altitude of seven thousand feet, it was surrounded by mountain ranges. The riders fixed a stare as they passed the sprawling governor's palace, and the newly erected tall, granite monument commemorating the Civil War, dead in the center of the town plaza. It had become a local landmark of sorts.

Across the plaza, the distinctive two-story, red brick building with green trim marked the Sante Fe office of Wells Fargo.

Passers-by stopped to gawk at the strange little procession. In the lead was a tall man wearing buckskin pants under a long linen duster and riding a brown and white pinto gelding. He sat his saddle determinedly, stoically. The rider's dusty gray hat, wide brimmed with an open crown tilted low, partially hid the sky-blue eyes that fixed straight ahead, seemingly unaware of the onlooker's stares.

Behind him on a short lead was a floppy-eared mule with a heavy packsaddle. Trotting beside the buckskin was a large wolf dog whose head swung constantly from side to side, his dark eyes taking in every detail of his surroundings. Farther back rode two other fellows in dust covered suits that hardly drew a glance from the onlookers.

Jedidiah's eyes roamed the dusty street seeking the livery but saw mostly saloons instead.

"Either of you gents know where the livery is?" he asked over a shoulder.

"Straight ahead on the right," detective Hume offered reluctantly.

That fellow's shore got a burr under his saddle about something or other, Jedidiah told himself.

Finding the livery, he reined up under an open shed. He swept a gaze at the clean stalls that lined one side of the livery and was pleased. Climbing stiffly from the saddle, he handed his reins to the crippled up old Mexican fellow that hobbled forward. Detective Hume and Honeycutt did likewise.

"My mounts are used up," Jedidiah told the man, untying his saddlebags and swinging them across a shoulder. "A double measure of grain for my two and an extra dollar if you'll stall the pinto and rub him down good. My dog will be staying with my horse."

Jedidiah slid his Henry rifle from the backward saddleboot as his two companions made arrangements for their own horses.

"Bueno hombres," the old timer said, a crooked grin breaking across his weathered face. "I will treat your horses as I would my own."

While he waited on his two traveling companions, Jedidiah rolled himself a smoke and flicked a glance at the fading sunset. Even as he watched, it gently kissed the western mountaintop, quickly died for the day and was buried somewhere beyond the distant horizon.

He was bone tired. A good meal and a soft bed shore would go good right now. It had been a hard fifty mile ride across the mountains between his Angel Fire home and Sante Fe.

"Dog," Jedidiah said softly to the big animal as if he were speaking to a child. "Stay."

The three men strode side by side down the dusty street toward the two-story hotel. A breeze fluttered Jedidiah's long duster. Little plumes of dust puffed away from their boot heels as they walked and were swept eastward by a hot wind.

Spurs jingling, they pushed through the door of the Grand Hotel. A bald headed little desk clerk with a sallow complexion barely spared a glance over the top of a newspaper as they entered. He didn't seem at all pleased for the interruption and went back to his reading, ignoring their presence.

"We'll be needing three rooms," Jedidiah said, plopping his rifle on top of the counter loudly.

Clearly annoyed, the desk clerk slowly pushed to his feet. Over the rims of his tiny spectacles he looked at the rifle, then up into the eyes of the tall man staring back at him. Something he saw in those eyes caused his own to wall white. He hurriedly handed Jedidiah the ink quill and spun the registration book for him to sign his name.

"Yes...yes, sir," he stammered, twisting to grab three keys, dropped one, and retrieved it quickly. "Would there be anything else, sir?"

"Is Mr. Winston Taylor registered?" detective Hume asked.

"Yes sir!" the fellow said proudly. "You must be the gentlemen he has been expecting. He said when you arrived to tell you he'd be pleased if you would join him for dinner at eight o'clock at the Sante Fe Café. It's over on the next street and to your right."

"Where might a fellow arrange for a bath?" Jedidiah asked, scooping up his rifle and a key.

"You'll find bath stalls right out back," the little man said, suddenly overly helpful. "I'll be more than happy to instruct Juanitta to prepare a hot bath if you like."

"You do that. I'll stash my stuff in the room and be out shortly. Don't know about you boys," Jedidiah told his two companions, "but I'm gonna wash off some of this trail dust before supper. Whatta you say we just meet over at the restaurant at eight?"

"I'm gonna wet my whistle at that saloon across the street," James Hume mumbled as he snatched his key from the desk clerk's hand.

"Think I'll tag along with you," his partner told him.

Jedidiah found room number four and pushed inside. It wasn't much bigger than a good size horse stall. It contained only a bed, a washstand with a blue-speckled pitcher and washbasin, and a single straight chair. He propped his Henry rifle beside the bed, checked the sheets, and tossed his saddlebags on the bed.

Unbuckling the strap to the bags, he withdrew one of the two rolled up bundles of clean clothes Minnie had packed for him. From past experience he knew the tightly wound roll would contain underclothes, socks, shirt, and britches, all rolled up and tied with a rawhide pigging string.

With the roll of clothes tucked under one arm and his straight razor in his hand, he stepped to the single window and lifted a curled finger to push aside the faded curtain. He peered through the dirty glass at the settling darkness. The North Star winked its companions awake and punched light holes in the velvety canopy that had captured the countryside.

Jedidiah knew that back at the cabin, Mose and Minnie would be sitting on the front porch, most likely looking up at those same stars. Mose would be sipping a second or third cup of coffee and smoking that old corncob pipe of his. Minnie would be snapping beans or darning socks and singing that Rock of Ages song as she rocked back and forth in that old straw-bottomed chair.

They were like family. Like his papa, and his papa's papa, Mose had been with the Boone family all his life. Jedidiah looked on him like a brother. In lots of ways, he was closer to the big black man than he was to any of his own four brothers.

His thoughts were scattered by a heavily loaded freight wagon drawn by six tired looking horses lumbering down the street, undoubtedly nearing the end of a long haul from somewhere.

The driver most likely had a wife and kids waiting supper on him. That would be nice. Jedidiah shook the thought from his mind, turned abruptly and headed out the door.

He found the bath stalls out back of the hotel and was greeted warmly by an attractive young Mexican señorita that couldn't have been more than eighteen.

"Do you speak English?" Jedidiah asked awkwardly.

"Si, señor," she replied, handing him a bar of soap and a towel. "My name is Juanitta. I will help you with your bath."

She pulled open a curtain on the first booth and stood aside for him to enter. He hesitated. The slightest hint of a smile creased her lips as she noticed his embarrassment.

"Don't reckon I need any help to take a bath," he told her.

"Then I will return in half an hour," she said, flashing a pretty smile.

He stepped inside and waited until she closed the curtain before undressing. A thin vapor of steam rose from the large, round, wooden tub. Leaning over, he gingerly tested it with a finger, then slowly climbed inside. The hot water felt heavenly.

As he soaked, he thought about why he was here. Wonder what Winston's got on his mind? Must be mighty important for him to come all the way from San Francisco just to meet with me. How long has it been since I've seen him? Close to a year I reckon. It'll be good to see him again.

Jedidiah pushed through the door of the Sante Fe Café and swept the large room with a searching glance. His entrance drew only a few looks from a scattering of locals, drummers, and cowboys that occupied half of the dozen tables in the place. Most were too busy filling their bellies to give him a second glance.

The two detectives, Hume and Honeycutt, had already arrived

and were sitting at a corner table with Winston Taylor. Jedidiah headed that way.

Winston didn't seem to have changed much in the year or so since he had seen him. Even without the uniform, a blind man could tell he was every bit a military man. Tall, square shouldered, well built. A shock of dark hair was well trimmed and neatly combed. He sat a chair the same way he rode a horse, erect and alert, his brown eyes taking in every detail, probing every movement. He spotted Jedidiah and snapped to his feet.

"Jedidiah," the businessman greeted, extending a hand. "That life of leisure doesn't seem to have hurt you any. It's good to see you again."

"Howdy, Winston," Jedidiah replied, taking the offered hand in a firm handshake. "It's been awhile."

"Way too long to my way of thinking," the businessman said, releasing Jedidiah's hand, motioning him toward an empty chair and filling his own.

Hume and Honeycutt glanced back and forth between each other and seemed bewildered as Jedidiah lifted out a chair and folded into it.

"You didn't tell me you already knew Mr. Taylor," Hume complained.

"Don't recall you asking," Jedidiah replied.

"Jedidiah and I served together in the war," the Wells Fargo executive explained. "We've been up and down the trail together more times than I care to remember. You ever think of the old days, Jedidiah?"

"Yeah, now and again. We had some high times, didn't we?"

The waitress came and poured coffee for everyone before taking their orders. Small talk occupied the time until their steaks arrived and for half an hour during the meal. The food was passable. Afterward, they relaxed over an after dinner cup.

"So," Jedidiah asked, unable to contain his curiosity any longer. "What brings you all the way from San Francisco?"

"I'd like for you to take a little ride with me in the morning. How about meeting me at the livery at first light?"

"You want us to ride along?" detective Hume asked anxiously, shooting a quick glance at his partner.

"Not this trip," Winston told him. "You two boys just stay close and we'll talk later in the day."

"Yes sir," Hume replied, pushing out of his chair. "It's still early. Think I'll knock down a nightcap before I turn in. Come on, Honeycutt. You owe me a drink."

Jedidiah watched the two detectives over the lip of his coffee cup as they strode from the room.

"That fellow seems a might itchy," he commented.

"Hume?" Winston said, glancing at his employees as they pushed out the door. "Oh, he's all right. He fancies himself something of a gun hand. They're both pretty fair detectives, though."

Jedidiah and Winston spent another hour reminiscing about their adventures in the war before saying goodnight. Not a word was spoken about the reason they were there. Jedidiah figured his friend would explain what was on his mind in his own good time.

Dawn crept silently over Sante Fe. A gentle blending of blue-gray pushed aside the dark velvety canopy of night and swallowed up the myriad of stars. Yellowish patches of light from coal oil lamps cast checker board squares along the dusty street.

Somewhere a rooster crowed. A dozen replies answered quickly and added music to the miracle birth of another day. A dog barked and the rhythmic beat of a blacksmith's hammer joined the chorus. The town was coming alive. Jedidiah loved the early mornings.

He strode down the deserted street with measured steps. A long linen duster mostly hid his buckskin britches and shirt. One side of the duster was hooked behind the bone handle Colt that rested in a greased cutaway holster tied low on his right leg. A Henry rifle dangled loosely from his left hand and a saddlebag rested over his shoulder.

Dog crawled to his feet in the pinto's stall and trotted to meet him as Jedidiah approached the shed. He paused to squat and ruffle the dog's hair and pat him on the head.

"Didn't know whether to feed him or not," the old holster said as he limped forward with a feed bucket in his hand. "Kind of afraid to get too close. I get the idea he'd tear a man's arm plumb off."

"Don't want him fed," Jedidiah said. "Don't want him getting use to taking handouts. He looks out for himself."

"I've got Mr. Taylor's mount saddled and waiting," the old liveryman said. "He sent word he'd be riding out early, at first light."

"Then I reckon he's late," Jedidiah commented as he led Butternut from the stall and threw a saddle on him.

"Who's late?" Winston asked, strolling up.

"Never knowed you to be on time in all the years we rode together," Jedidiah joshed. "You'll likely be late for your own funeral."

"Sure hope so."

Jedidiah toed a stirrup and swung into the saddle. Winston spurred a big, rawboned sorrel up beside him and they rode stirrup to stirrup as they had so many times in the past.

"You haven't changed a bit," Jedidiah commented as they rode up the street. "You still sit a saddle like a sitting hen on a nest full of eggs afraid you might break one."

"I can still out ride you seven ways to Sunday," Winston shot back at his friend. "Is that wolf going with us?"

"He's only half wolf," Jedidiah said. "He goes everywhere I go."

"Sure hope he knows I'm a friend."

"Where we headed?" Jedidiah asked as they left the edge of town behind them and headed south into the desert countryside.

"There's a horse ranch about six miles ahead. That's where we're headed. I'll explain when we get there."

* * *

The red sun peeked over the eastern horizon and sent its spiked rays racing across the desert. Within minutes it warmed the white sand and sent heat waves radiating upward. Only the soft crunching of the horse's hooves, the steady creaking of saddle leather and an occasional snort from one of their mounts broke the early morning desert stillness.

Cresting a low hill, they reined up. They sat their horses, and peered down into a beautiful little green valley with a stream creasing its middle. A high wall surrounded a sprawling adobe hacienda. Several large barns with pole corrals stood nearby. It was an impressive layout.

"That place belonged to Benjamin Fargo. He lived there with his wife, Henrietta, and their two girls. Eleven-year-old Elizabeth and five-year-old Rebecca."

"What happened to them?"

"Don't know for sure. The sheriff says it was Indians. It happened about three weeks ago. A neighbor was riding by and spotted the buzzards circling. They didn't just kill them. They butchered the father and mother as well as a half dozen workers.

"They found the Mexican vaqueros still in their bunks, their throats slashed from ear to ear. Ben Fargo's stomach had been slit open and his intestines strewn around the kitchen. The sheriff says he was most likely still alive at the time. He had been scalped too.

"They did unspeakable things to his wife. When they got through with her they cut off her breasts and slit her throat."

"What about the two girls?" Jedidiah asked, already suspecting the answer before he asked the question.

"Not a trace of them," Winston told him. "The sheriff speculates the Indians took them captive."

"Was this fellow part of the, Fargo, as in Wells Fargo?"

"Benjamin was William G. Fargo's younger brother. Mr. Fargo is now president of the entire Wells Fargo Company.

"I see," Jedidiah said, expelling a slow slide of air. "Let me guess. I'm supposed to get the girls back, right?"

"Right."

"Winston, you realize I've got about as much chance doing that as a billy goat sprouting wings. Even if I could find 'em, which ain't likely, the odds against them still being alive are more than I can count."

"But will you try?" his friend's voice had a pleading sound to it.

For a long space of time Jedidiah sat his saddle, fingered an earlobe, and stared off at nothing.

Winston sat silently, knowing his friend was struggling within himself, weighing the problems and the possibilities, not wanting to say no, but afraid of saying yes.

"Let's ride down and take a look around," Jedidiah finally said, touching heels to Butternut's tender flanks, "but I ain't promising nothing, mind you?"

"I understand. What do you expect to find after three weeks?" Winston asked as they approached the large hacienda. "The sheriff said he went over the whole area with a fine-tooth comb."

"Most likely nothing, but we'll never know till we look."

They looped reins around the hitching post near the front entrance to the walled compound and strode through the open gate. The large courtyard was filled with flowering azaleas, blooming cactus, and yucca plants. A winding path, interrupted by two log benches, circled the garden. It was an impressive place.

Jedidiah's eyes flicked from side to side, absorbing every detail of the large hacienda, searching every corner, looking for something, anything, that shouldn't be there, something that didn't fit the character of the house.

The place had been ransacked. Drawers pulled out, clothes strewn about, furniture overturned. He knew there would be nothing of value left behind. The sand scrubbed wooden floor of the kitchen was discolored by two large dried pools of blood and testified to unfathomable acts of brutality.

"According to the sheriff, they found Benjamin here near the outside door," Winston explained. "He figured the ones that did it must have been waiting outside when Ben unbarred and opened it that morning. Henrietta was over there in the corner. Her clothes had all been ripped off and there were signs she had been raped repeatedly. They cut off her breasts. Why would they do that, Jedidiah? Why would they do something like that?"

"They make pouches from the skin of a woman's breast. They hang them from a rawhide cord around their neck. It's a status thing, like having a scalp hanging from their belt."

"That's horrible!" Winston exclaimed. "That's inhuman! What kind of man would do that to another human being?"

"An Apache," Jedidiah replied absently.

Jedidiah stood, silently staring at the blood discolored spots on the floor. His finger and thumb tugged at his right earlobe, his mind lost in deep thought.

"There's something bad wrong here," he told his friend. "This was done by Apaches sure enough, but there's something about it that's got me bum fuzzled."

"So?" Winston asked, not understanding what his friend was getting at. "This whole area of New Mexico Territory is crawling with Apache. What's unusual about that?"

"Just like the United States is made up of separate states, each with their own state lines defining their boundaries. Each state is then divided into different counties, each with their own county lines.

"Well, the same is true with the Apache Nation. It is divided into twenty-four separate and distinct groups. Each of those groups is then subdivided into tribes. Each of those tribes and groups has their own boundaries, which they guard jealously. It is a serious infraction for one group or tribe to cross into another's territory. It often is the cause of war between tribes.

"Each of those groups and tribes also have their own customs and traditions that identify them from all the others, sort of like a trademark or calling card. This massacre was the handiwork of the Chokonen tribe of the Chiricahua Apache. The chief is a renegade named Cochise.

"Remember what they're calling the "Bascom Affair" that happened back in '61?"

"Oh, yeah," Winston said. "Something about a young greenhorn lieutenant that accused some Apaches of stealing a young white boy. The lieutenant arrested and hung a bunch of them over near Fort Bowie, wasn't it?"

"That's the one. The Apache he tried to arrest was Cochise. Turned out he wasn't the one that done it. That stupid act started a war that's still going on to this day. They say Cochise and two hundred or so followers are holed up somewhere in the Dragoon Mountains. The army's been searching for them several months but, so far, haven't been able to flush them out. That's four hundred miles southwest of here."

"So, let me see if I'm understanding you," Winston asked, rubbing his chin. "Are you saying this was done by Cochise and his men?"

"No, that's the thing that's strange about it. Oh, it's their trademark sure enough, no doubt about it. They're the only Apache that's known to slit their victims' belly open and string the intestines all over the place like that. They're also the only ones I ever heard about that use a woman's breasts to make their medicine pouches.

"But the thing is they would never come this far north to raid. First off, they'd be crossing the territorial lines of several other groups. They'd never do that. Second, it's clear from the tracks I saw coming in, they stole a bunch of horses and headed them south. There's no way they're gonna drive stolen horses four hundred miles. If they're gonna steal horses, they could do it a whole lot closer to their hideout.

"Even allowing they did ride this far north to make a raid, why here? Why this particular ranch? They must have passed a hundred places that had horses, and why didn't they burn the place down like they always do?"

"So what are you suggesting then?"

It took a long minute before Jedidiah answered.

"I don't rightly know," Jedidiah told his friend honestly. "Something just don't add up. It don't seem right. I can't put my finger on it, but...it just smells funny."

A hundred miles to the south, in a small hut among a cluster of adobe shanties scattered along the Rio Hondo River high in the El Capitan Mountains, Rebecca Fargo clung to her older sister. She lifted her dirty, tear-streaked face to stare through red, swollen eyes at Elizabeth.

Her breath came in jerky spasms. Fear flavored every word. Her eyes puddled with tears."Wh...what are they gonna do to us?" she stammered. "Are the ugly men gonna hurt us?"

Until she heard the terror in her sister's voice Elizabeth, herself, had been smothered in her own grief, held captive to her own fears. Suddenly she realized she was the older one here. Like it or not, she was now responsible for her sister. She must say something to reassure Rebecca, but what?

With no small difficulty she closed her eyes and waited for her heart to stop pounding in her throat, for her legs to stop quivering.

"Shh..." Elizabeth placed a finger across her lips. "They might hear you."

"Will daddy come and take us back home?" Rebecca whispered.

The fear and confusion in Rebecca's voice swelled the ache around Elizabeth's heart. She didn't answer right away, she couldn't. How could she explain to her little sister their daddy wouldn't be coming? What could she possibly say that would offer some measure of hope? How could she explain what she had seen as they were being carried from their home? How could she begin to explain why their parents were killed when she didn't understand it herself? Rebecca must never know the awful things they had done to their father and mother.

Elizabeth's stomach did flip-flops and bitter bile surged into her throat every time she remembered the unspeakable scene in the kitchen of their home. She would never forget it. The memory of it would haunt her until the day she died.

After their capture they had been slung across a horse in front of an Indian. They had ridden most of the morning, hid in a wooded canyon until dark, then ridden all night. The next two days were like the first. Riding all night, hiding during the day, then riding again.

She had no earthly idea where they were. She only knew they were a long way from home and her parents were both dead, and she and Becky probably soon would be. Until then, Elizabeth knew she must try to keep her little sister as calm as she could.

"It's going to be all right, Becky," she promised, drawing a shaky breath and wishing she could believe her own words.

"Try not to cry. Daddy will find us."

Elizabeth hugged her sister close, swaying in the age-old rhythm she had learned in her mother's arms. Rebecca buried her face in Elizabeth's shoulder, sobbing as if her heart would break. Sunlight slanted through a crack in the door of the single room of the adobe hut where they had been held since their capture. The heat was stifling. The air hung thick with the smell of dust and sweat and fear. The stench from their own excrement drifted from a corner where they relieved themselves, and stung Elizabeth's nostrils.

Just then an old Indian woman swung the door open. In her hands she carried two bowls of pasty something that had become their daily ration. The woman spoke broken English and had told Elizabeth earlier her name was Two Deers Running. Her once a day visits had become a time Elizabeth looked forward to. On several occasions she had tried to question the woman about what was going to happen to them but had met with only stony silence.

Their nightgowns had been replaced with soft, deerskin dresses with a fringe around the sleeves and hem. The old woman had brought moccasins for their feet and a blanket apiece for their beds.

"You eat," she said, sitting the bowls in front of them.

Other than Two Deers Running, only two other people had come to the little hut where they were being held. One was the tall Indian that had taken them from their home. He was the leader of the group that raided their ranch. He was ugly and the cause of both her and Rebecca's reoccurring nightmares.

The other man had come to their hut only once. He was a man Two Deers Running was very scared of. She spoke his name only once in a frightened whisper—Scarface. He seemed to be part Indian and part white man. He was tall, heavily muscled, and had a long scar that started at the corner of his eye and ended at a twisted lip.

"When can we go home?" Elizabeth asked the woman.

Two Deers Running only shook her head sadly and hurried from the room, locking the door behind her.

"Let's rein up here at the Wells Fargo office," Winston Taylor told Jedidiah as they rode into Sante Fe. "There's someone I want you to meet."

They looped reins over a hitching post and pushed through the door of the two-story red brick building with green trim. The sign over the door identified it as the Wells Fargo Agency.

A young clerk with a green eyeshade straightened behind a high counter as they entered. An armed guard eyed them searchingly from his post near the front door.

Winston led the way to a stairway attached to the wall and climbed the stairs quickly. Jedidiah followed. At the top, they turned left along a hallway to a closed door. Winston knocked and paused, waiting until he heard a voice from inside before opening the door.

The room was a large office with a connecting door that Jedidiah could see led to an adjoining bedroom. A large desk sat before a window that faced the street. At the desk sat a large, distinguished looking man with a full beard and dressed in a business suit. He rose to his feet as they entered.

"Jedidiah, I want you to meet the President of the Wells Fargo Agency, Mr. William G. Fargo. Mr. Fargo, this is Jedidiah Boone."

The businessman came around his desk with a hand extended and a genuine looking smile showing through his neatly trimmed beard and mustache.

"Mr. Boone," he said in a deep voice. "It's my pleasure to meet you. Winston has told me a lot about you."

The businessman pumped Jedidiah's hand in a warm and firm handshake.

"It's good to make your acquaintance," Jedidiah said, feeling kind of intimidated by the businessman's presence.

"Have a seat," the Wells Fargo executive said in a friendly tone and pointed to two chairs as he folded into a big one behind his desk. "Would you like a cigar?"

"Thanks, but no, sir," Jedidiah told him, hooking his hat over a bent knee. "I never took up the habit." Only because I couldn't afford them, he thought to himself.

"We've just returned from the ranch," Winston hastened to explain. "Jedidiah made some fascinating discoveries."

"Oh?" Mr. Fargo asked, his interest immediately aroused.

"I'll let him explain," Winston said, swinging his gaze in Jedidiah's direction.

"Well, sir," Jedidiah said. "First off, I want to say how sorry I feel about the loss of your brother and his family. It's a terrible tragedy."

"Thank you, Mr. Boone. That's very nice of you."

"There's no doubt in my mind it was Apaches that done the

deed. There's something bothering me about the whole thing though. All the signs point to one particular tribe of the Chiricahua Apache. The trouble is, that tribe's territory is four hundred miles to the southwest. They're holed up in their stronghold in the Dragoon Mountains. There's no way they'd raid this far north."

The businessman steepled his fingers, intent on what was being said, his face displaying a contemplative expression.

"Are you saying that's the group who kidnapped my nieces?" Mr. Fargo asked.

"I can't rightly explain it just now," Jedidiah told him, "but it shore looks that way."

"Mr. Boone, Benjamin was the only brother I had. Our mother died giving him birth. Our father died a year later. I've never married. Those two nieces of mine are the only family I have in this world. I'll do anything to get them back safe.

"Winston tells me you've worked for Wells Fargo on a couple of special jobs in the past. He says you're the best tracker he's ever seen. Would you consider taking on this job for me?"

Jedidiah's features went stony. He looked down, studying the floor for a long moment. When he glanced up, his mouth was set in a tight line. His eyes locked with those of the big man. They were pleading eyes. Desperate eyes. They were the eyes of a man who was dying inside, who was about to lose everything that mattered in life. How could he say no?

"Mr. Fargo, I have to be honest with you. The chances of me finding the ones that did this are might-near impossible. They could be anywhere. More than that, even if I could find them, I've got to tell you, the chances of me getting them back alive...or getting out myself...well...there just ain't any."

"I can't give up, Mr. Boone!" Fargo came near shouting. "I won't give up! Until I know for sure they're not alive, I'll never stop searching. They're all I have."

What could he say? Could he blame the man? Wouldn't he do the same if they were his own family?

"Will you help me, Mr. Boone? Will you try to find them?"

For a long time Jedidiah stared off into space without answering. No one spoke to break the silence. Finally, having made up his mind, he lifted his head.

"Give me some time to think on it," he told the businessman as he rose to his feet and shook Mr. Fargo's hand. "I'll let you know later this afternoon."

Neither he nor Winston said a word as they descended the stairs and pushed through the front door into the street.

"I think you've already made up your mind," Winston finally said as they led their horses toward the livery. "You're going to take the job aren't you?"

"I'm leaning in that direction, Winston. Leaning hard. Guess I just have a hard time saying no when good people ask for help. I was never one to turn a deaf ear."

"You know this is a suicide mission, Jedidiah. A whole regiment couldn't go in there and get those girls back alive."

"No," Jedidiah agreed. "But one man might stand a chance. Not likely, but enough that I've got to give it a try."

Later that afternoon Jedidiah and Winston returned to the Wells Fargo office. William Fargo stood as they pushed through the door at his invitation. A worried, questioning look occupied his face.

"I'll do my best, sir," Jedidiah told him simply.

"Thank you, Mr. Boone. Thank you. You have my deepest gratitude. Winston will remain in Sante Fe until this matter is concluded. He will provide whatever you need. Winston, place those two detectives of yours at Mr. Boone's disposal. I understand Major Sheldon is the officer in charge at Fort Cummings. Arrange with him to assign a squad of soldiers to assist Mr. Boone."

"I appreciate the thought, Mr. Fargo, but I work alone," Jedidiah said.

"But surely you'll need help. They'll only be there to assist you, I assure you," The businessman pressed.

"Mr. Fargo," Jedidiah said. "With all due respect, sir, it's gonna be a full time job just trying to stay alive out there, much less having to explain every move I make to somebody. No, I go alone or I don't go."

"Very well then," Fargo said, accepting Jedidiah's judgment. "Winston will arrange to pay you generously for your time and expenses, of course, and there'll be a five thousand dollar reward for each of the girls you bring back alive and well. If there's anything else you require, just let Winston know."

"I ain't doing this for the money, Mr. Fargo," Jedidiah said, pushing to his feet.

"Nevertheless that would be a small price to pay to have them returned safely."

"Is there anything more you need?" Winston asked. "Is there anything I can do to help?"

The two friends stood in the dusty street in front of the General Mercantile. They had spent an hour talking with the sheriff, going over every detail of what he had found at the scene of the massacre when he arrived, but nothing he said added any more light on who might have done it or why.

Winston had helped load the trail supplies onto Jedidiah's pack mule. Now, it was time to say goodbye. Jedidiah shoved his newly purchased .52 caliber Sharps long rifle into the backward facing saddle boot and looped the rawhide thong connected to the handle of the ten gauge Stevens sawed-off double-barreled shotgun over his saddle horn.

He fixed his friend with a long stare.

"As a matter of fact there is," Jedidiah said. "If this don't work out right, I'd appreciate it if you'd see Mose and Minnie get what money I've got coming. Would you do that for me?"

For a long minute the two friends locked their looks on each other's eyes, each knowing this could well be their final goodbye. Winston Taylor reached a hand. Jedidiah took it. Their hands clasped, and held for a long minute.

Chapter Three

The trail was easy to follow, maybe too easy. Jedidiah picked it up at Benjamin Fargo's horse ranch and followed it until near dark. Reining up, he stepped from his horse and knelt beside the tracks. He dropped into an easy crouch, his back end resting comfortably on his boot heels.

For a long time he studied the tracks, tracing a finger lightly around their outlines, counting, studying even the smallest details. His practiced eyes read the sign as most men would read a newspaper. The trail was faint and windblown and only barely visible. Best he could tell after that much time, there were eight of them, two of the riders rode shod horses, six rode unshod ponies. The fact that they were driving two dozen shod horses stolen from the Fargo ranch made reading the signs more difficult.

He had maybe an hour and a half of daylight left. He knew he wouldn't get far before good dark but struck out anyway, feeling a need to make as much progress as possible. It was full dark when Dog found the wooded canyon where the kidnappers had camped and Jedidiah decided to make his own camp there for the night.

Building a small fire under a sprawling cedar to scatter the smoke, he put on a pot of coffee, fried salt pork, and sliced a potato into the pan. After a satisfying supper, he leaned back against his saddle with a cup of steaming coffee, closed his eyes and listened to the silence that surrounded him.

Dog lay beside him with his head nestled on his paws. Jedidiah knew that wouldn't last long. He knew the wolf half of the wild blood coursing through his veins would win out sometime during the night and the dog would disappear, only to return after he had satisfied his hunger.

Jedidiah sipped his coffee and stared up at a bright half-moon that shone through sparse clouds. Tiny blinking stars punched pinholes in the black canopy overhead. He was uneasy...uncomfortable...unsure of his ability to accomplish what he had set out to do...but feeling an unexplainable need to try. He felt a heavy sense of responsibility upon his shoulders he had seldom felt before, grave, constricting, overwhelming. He harbored no misconceptions about the impossibility of the undertaking, but knew he had to try anyway.

He slept fitfully and rose just minutes before the first gray fingers of false dawn crept silently across the dark canopy overhead. By first light he had finished his breakfast, and stomped out the fire, sending a fiery shower of sparks into the air.

"Let's go, Dog," he spoke softly to his furry companion.

The day broke clear and hot. The New Mexico sun bore down with a vengeance from an azure sky, cooking into the barren countryside. Spread out before him was a vast wasteland, golden and gleaming in the bright sunlight. He could see for miles. Buttes, plateaus, and mesas painted a pretty picture against a powder-blue sky. The light turned the shimmering heat waves into a rainbow of colors and distorted the distant horizon. Off in the distance a line of mountains reached lofty peaks into the sky.

The landscape through which he now rode was changing rapidly. Waist-high mesquite bushes with their gnarled, spindly limbs grew in groves that littered the sandy, rocky terrain. Cholla cactus with their dagger spines tore at the animals and Jedidiah's buckskin pants when he passed too close. He circled a scattered growth of juniper, prickly pear, and ocotillo. Above him a hawk rode lazy circles against the blue sky, then tilted its wings and angled off gracefully, continuing its never ending search for food.

The sun stood noon-high and stole all but the most meager patches of shade. The wind picked up, tearing in from the west and carrying with it the searing heat as if from hell itself. In minutes it swept the sandy ground clean, erasing any sign of passage as if it had never been there. Now there was no trail to follow. He could only continue south, the same direction they seemed to have been headed.

The sinking sun was still full-ball the following day when he reined up a couple of hundred yards shy of Hobbs Trading post. It was a large, log and mud shanty situated on a hill overlooking the fork where the Rio Salado merged into the Rio Grande River. Jedidiah wanted to talk with Amos Hobbs, the grizzled old trapper that owned the place. If there were a man alive that knew what was going on in this part of the country, it would be him.

Amos lived in this remote middle of nowhere with his Navaho squaw and their six half-breed children. Several of her relatives and hangers-on lived in tiny sod and log huts scattered around the trading post. They trapped along the rivers and traded beaver pelts for blankets, tobacco, cooking pots, and no telling what all else.

Hobbs Station was kind of like a safe haven for Indians of all tribes for a hundred miles around simply because the Indians all needed it for trade. It was the one place in the whole territory where they wouldn't kill each other on sight. Jedidiah allowed his searching gaze to crawl slowly over the surrounding area.

Four broomtails stood hipshot in a pole corral behind the trading post, swishing their tails at pesky horseflies. A dozen goats milled about, searching for anything that resembled food. Half as many large hounds lay sleeping on the shady side of the building.

Down along the riverbank, several half naked children ran and played, their happy laughter making a pleasant sound. He could see nothing that would suggest cause for alarm. Nevertheless, he raked the right side of his long duster behind the walnut handle of his .44 caliber Frontier model Colt tied low on his right leg and heeled his mount forward.

He got no closer than a hundred yards before the hounds picked up his scent and filled the late afternoon with a commotion that would have woke the dead. Almost immediately a huge mountain of a man stooped his head and stepped from the building with a double-barrel shotgun in his hand.

Amos Hobbs was big-mountain grizzly big .He would literally look down on Jedidiah's own height of one hand over six feet. The man's face barely showed under the full beard and mustache and long, stringy hair. Only his dark, flashing eyes peeked through all that hair and told any man with a lick of sense they might be wise to walk easy around this fellow. He wore dirty, rawhide britches held up by red suspenders over faded red long johns. His black, high-topped boots looked like they had been up and down way too many trails.

"Well I'll swun," the big man bellowed over the sound of the barking hounds. "Would you look what the wind blowed in? Howdy to you, Jedidiah."

"Howdy, Amos. It's been awhile."

"That it has, that it has. Spring was a year ago as I recollect. Shut up hounds!" he yelled.

The half dozen barking dogs reluctantly cowed down, trotted a few steps away, and give it another try. Amos picked up a nearby rock and sent it flying at the nearest. It yelped, and scurried off around the building. Its companions followed.

"Don't know why I keep them around," the trapper complained. "They ain't fit for nothing but to make noise and eat me out of house and home. See you still got that wolf dog tagging along with you. As I recall, the last time you rode through, that critter killed three or four of my best hounds."

"They shouldn't have messed with him," Jedidiah said simply, flicking a glance at the big animal standing motionless beside the buckskin, eyeing the hounds. "He don't like to be messed with."

"Can't rightly say I blame him none," Amos Hobbs said, arming away a trickle of tobacco juice from his chin and leaning the shotgun against the log building. "Kind of that way myself, I reckon. What you doing way down this way? Kind of long way from your stomping grounds, ain't it?"

"Looking for two white girls," Jedidiah told him, swinging leadenly to the ground and squatting onto his haunches with Butternut's reins still laced between a thumb and fingers.

As he said it his gaze searched for and found the dark, flashing eyes buried among all that hair. He watched intently, looking for any reaction, any nervousness, any hint of knowledge the trapper's eyes might reveal. He saw nothing.

"About four weeks or so ago some Indians raided a horse ranch just south of Sante Fe. They killed half dozen vaqueros while they were still in their bunks. They waited until first light when the man opened the house up. When he did, they slit open his belly and strung his guts all over the kitchen. They raped the woman, cut off both of her breasts, and then slit her throat.

"The couple had two girls, one eleven, the other barely five. Looks like the Indians took them captive. When they left, they took a couple of dozen horses and anything in the house that was worth taking. They didn't torch the house. They left it standing."

As Jedidiah was talking the big trapper sat down in the dirt and leaned his back against the wall of the trading post. When Jedidiah finished, Amos Hobbs didn't speak for a long space of time.

"Don't make no sense," the big trapper said. "All you told me points a finger square at Cochise and his men, but that just ain't likely at all. He's holed up in the Dragoon Mountains two hundred miles to the southeast. He shore ain't gonna ride all the way to Sante Fe just to steal a few horses and a couple of kids.

"Besides that, he's got his hands full fighting the army. I doubt he's gonna risk stirring up the other Apache tribes against him by raiding in their territory. Another thing, I never heard of them raiding a place and not burning it down. If you ask me, the whole thing stinks to high heaven. Something ain't right about it."

"That's what I thought, too," Jedidiah said, still searching the trapper's eyes. "You haven't heard anything about two white girls have you?"

"Not a word," Amos Hobbs told him, returning the unwavering stare with one of his own.

"I'd tell you if I had. I'll keep my ears open though."

Five, stair-stepped, bronze-skinned children straggled from the direction of the river toward the door of the trading post. A dozen others scattered to the nearby shanties as the sun settled behind the western horizon.

"You still just got six?" Jedidiah asked, tousling the midnight black hair of the youngest as he passed. The boy looked to be no more than three.

"Nope," Amos said, taking a deep inhale from his pipe and blowing it skyward in a long, blue tendril of smoke. "Seven, and another on the way. Those Navaho women are good for making babies. You ought to get you one. Running Deer's got a sister right over yonder in one of those huts. Just say the word and I'll have her fetched. You can bed her for the night or take her home with you, whatever suits your fancy."

"Don't think so," Jedidiah said, "but thanks for the offer."

"One thing about those two white girls you're looking for," the trapper volunteered. "You said the oldest was eleven, didn't you? You don't have to worry about some Apache laying with them for a while."

"Oh," Jedidiah said, his head coming up with interest. "How's that?"

"Cause they won't bother a girl until she becomes a woman, until she starts bleeding. The oldest one's most likely got another few months or so. You don't find her by then she'll be the wife of some young buck and you ain't got a snowballs chance in hell of getting her back."

"What will they likely do with them?" Jedidiah wanted to know.

"Who knows? They might keep them and raise them as their own, although that ain't likely with them at war. They might sell them down in Mexico for prostitution or..."

The words hung in the rapidly graying air like a dark cloud and had the hint of something even more dreadful, more sinister, than what he had already suggested.

"Or what?" Jedidiah asked, not sure he was ready for the answer. "What could possibly be worse?"

"Or...they might sell them to the Comanchero," Amos Hobbs said in a hoarse whisper, dropping his head as he said it. "They're worse than the vultures around here. They're the scum of the earth."

"They ever come around?" Jedidiah asked.

"Ever now and then. I don't cotton to 'em. I don't trust 'em no further than I could throw that mule of yours."

"Well, I'd best be going, I reckon," Jedidiah said, lifting to his full height and hooking a boot in a stirrup. "I've got it in mind to make camp just down river a piece unless you know a reason why not."

"No reason," the trader said, "You're welcome to stay for supper. The woman makes a right good rabbit stew."

Jedidiah shifted to get comfortable in his saddle and did a half hitch of Mule's lead rope around the saddle horn.

"I'll be moseying on. If you hear anything, I'd be obliged if you'd get me word."

"Which way you headed, Jedidiah?"

"Don't seem to me I got much choice. We both agree it was the Chokonen tribe of the Chiricahua Apache that took the girls. If they got 'em, I've got to try to get them back. That means I've got to find Cochise."

"You don't look like a crazy man, but that's shore what you are if you're thinking about riding into the Dragoon Mountains looking for Cochise and his renegades. Jedidiah, they'll slit your belly and scatter your guts all over them mountains and laugh all the time they're doing it."

"Maybe so," Jedidiah allowed, "but I've got to try. I promised a friend."

"That's one promise you're liable to wish you'd never made. If you're bound and determined to head southwest, I'd be obliged if you'd look in on a greenhorn family that's settled a piece of land about ten miles in the direction you're headed."

"What in the world are they doing out there?" Jedidiah asked.

"They came through here with a wagon train couple of months ago headed for Colorado. Two of his girls took sick and they couldn't go on. The train waited awhile then went on without them. The girls died later on.

"This farmer is bound and determined he's gonna stay where he buried his girls. Says he's gonna farm. He's gonna get his whole family killed is what he's gonna do. They'll be buried right alongside his two girls."

"Is the man touched in the head?" Jedidiah asked, disbelieving anybody could be so dumb as to try to settle land smack-dab in the middle of Apache territory.

"He shore ain't none too smart, to my way of thinking. He's got a stubborn streak as wide as Texas," Amos Hobbs said. "Nice family. A good looking wife and a full-growed daughter that's as pretty as I've ever seen. He's got two strapping boys that's might near as big as he is. Dag-blamed shame. He's gonna get 'em all killed dead."

"I'll look in on 'em," Jedidiah said, shaking his head and clucking Butternut forward. "Let's go, Dog."

"You take care of that sandy-colored scalp of yours," the big trader hollered after him. "Some Apache buck would love having that hanging from his belt."

Jedidiah lifted his hand in acknowledgment and farewell.

He was restless, uneasy. He knew he couldn't sleep and he wasn't all that hungry so he kept riding southwest. He thought about the two captives, Elizabeth and Rebecca. Wonder where they are right now? Reckon they're even still alive? If they are, what must they be going through?

He knew it was an impossible mission he had embarked upon. Even if by some stroke of luck he could do what the army hadn't been able to do and find Cochise, what made him think the Apache chief wouldn't do what Amos Hobbs said he would do—string his guts all over the Dragoon Mountains? Still, he knew he had to try.

What about that pilgrim farmer? Jedidiah thought. That fellow needed to have his head examined, bringing his family way out here. If the Apaches hadn't found them yet, they soon would, and they would all die a pitiful death.

The country Jedidiah was riding through wasn't as desert-like as he had been in the past few days. Trees were plentiful and grass was green and thick. Numerous small creeks laced the countryside. He could see how a stranger to these parts might look at the land and decide it would be a good place to settle down and build a future for him and his family. But all this country held for somebody like that was an early grave.

Jedidiah glanced up at the thumbnail moon. The Big Dipper said it was near midnight. He decided he'd best make camp and try to get some shut-eye. Up ahead he spotted a little stream with a grove of cottonwood saplings straddling it. He headed for it.

Within half an hour he had seen to his animals and had coffee going. He figured a cup would go down really good to help wash down the beef jerky he planned to make out on for a late supper. The horses were hobbled on good graze and Dog had disappeared into the darkness. Jedidiah settled down against his saddle, blew the steam from his coffee, and nibbled on a piece of jerky.

The distant crack of a rifle wrenched Jedidiah from a sound sleep. He sat upright even as the sound of a volley of shots reached him in a burst of sharp, snapping sounds that filled the first grayness of a new day.

In short minutes he had Mule's packsaddle in place, Butternut's saddle cinched tight, and had swung hurriedly into the saddle. He kicked his pinto into a run toward the shooting that had now slowed to a sporadic scattering of shots.

The sky lightened and beyond the next rise he could see a long tendril of smoke feathering skyward, bent sharply by a westerly wind. It wasn't large enough or black enough to be a house fire. It had to be smoke from the greenhorn farmer's breakfast fire.

Jedidiah topped the long rise at full gallop. Mule struggled to keep pace with the long legged pinto. In the valley below, Jedidiah's quick sweeping gaze revealed a half built log cabin, whose walls stood only chest high. Two covered wagons sat nearby. A pole corral held half a dozen horses, two milk cows and a bull.

Off to the left he counted nine riders. They were bunched near a grove of sycamore beside a creek that lay a couple of hundred yards in front of the cabin. It looked to him like they were getting ready for another attack on the cabin.

Suddenly they wheeled their horses and headed straight for the cabin, firing as they rode. White puffs of gun smoke blossomed from the defenders hunkered down behind the half built walls. The pilgrim farmer was making quite a stand for himself.

Dropping the lead rope to Mule, Jedidiah buried his heels in the pinto's flanks and charged down the hill at full gallop to intercept the attackers. A closer look brought a moment of surprise; the attackers weren't Indians at all. They were Mexican and Americans. Comanchero! Jedidiah thought. The scourge of the whole New Mexico Territory. That farmer and his family are in a heap of trouble.

Reaching a hand, he threaded the leather thong attached to the sawed-off double barrel over his left wrist and thumbed back both hammers. Shifting Butternut's reins into the same hand, his right hand snaked his Henry rifle from its saddle boot. Working the lever with one hand, he snapped his wrist and let the weight of the barrel do the rest of the work, chambering a .44 shell into place.

The attackers peeled off into two groups, each group charging their horses past the partially built cabin on two sides, firing as they rode, obviously intending to surround the defenders. Their plan most likely would have worked too, if Jedidiah hadn't showed up.

Jedidiah was close and riding full out before they spotted him. Throwing up the rifle and aiming it like a pistol, he found the big chest with crisscrossed bandoleers of a bearded attacker. He pointed and fired. A finger of bright flame exploded from the nose of his rifle. The Comanchero spun crazily out of the saddle, twisting in midair, arms and legs askew.

Twirling the Henry, he levered another shell, found a new target, and touched the trigger. A rider in a big sombrero rolled over his galloping horse's rump, arms flailing the air.

Calmly Jedidiah worked the lever as he sped directly toward them, fired, levered, and fired again. He was upon them. A hatless rider on a red sorrel twisted in his saddle and swung a pistol in Jedidiah's direction. Red blossomed from the nose of the man's gun. The swish of a slug sped past Jedidiah's ear and sounded like a humming bird in flight. Jedidiah raised his left arm and touched the trigger of the sawed-off shotgun. The explosion radiated up his arm and rocked his shoulder like the kick of a mule. The blast lifted the man clear of his saddle like he had suddenly sprouted wings. A splay of blood, bone, and flesh showered through the air. The Comanchero was dead before his body hit the ground.

All around him Jedidiah could hear guns exploding. A slug tore past his middle, creasing his hip before slamming into the cantle of his saddle. Another slug whistled overhead, knifing through the air only inches above his head.

A rider charged him, spurring his big dun horse in a head-on assault. A blast from the other barrel of Jedidiah's shotgun hit the Comanchero like the wrath of God, taking out both horse and rider. The animal's front legs folded under him, pitching the faceless rider over the front of the horse in a headlong dive into eternity.

Jedidiah jerked his pinto around sharply, his gaze sweeping back and forth, searching for another target, and holding a tight rein on his frightened mount. All around him riderless horses trailing latigo trotted to a stop, snorting, legs shaking, ears flicking back and forth.

A bearded Comanchero spurred his mount through the door opening of the cabin, a pistol in his hand swung downward toward a target even as his horse reared. Jedidiah threw his rifle to his shoulder, sighted quickly down the barrel, and squeezed off a shot. The slug spun the man sideways, tearing the pistol from his fist. Working the lever, Jedidiah fired again. His second shot hit him square on, knocking him from the saddle.

Only two Comanchero were still in their saddles and obviously having had enough, they wheeled their mounts and lit out. As they sloshed into the stream a hundred yards away, Jedidiah pulled his buckskin to a stop, rose to his full height in the stirrups, and brought the Henry to a shoulder. He found his target and fired. A Mexican reeled from his saddle, tossing his rifle in the air as he plunged into the water.

Only one attacker remained, and he was whipping his mount up the long, sloping hill beyond the creek. Another fifty yards and he would disappear over the crest of the distant hill. Jedidiah couldn't let that happen. He must not get away.

Vaulting from his saddle, Jedidiah slid the Henry into its saddle boot and withdrew the Sharps .52 caliber buffalo gun from its reverse scabbard under the left saddle fender. He dropped to one knee and pulled the slipknot in the rawhide pigging string that held a small leather pouch to the handle of the big long rifle. Dumping half the contents on the ground, he scooped up one of the cartridges, opened the loading gate, and thumbed the big shell into place. Slamming the gate closed he brought the big rifle to shoulder and sighted down the long barrel.

Three or four more jumps and the Comanchero would be out of sight. Jedidiah guessed it to be a quarter of a mile shot. He laid the front sight square in the fleeing rider's back, then adjusted upward slightly, allowing for the distance. He took a deep breath, let it out in a long, slow slide, waited another stride for the rider to crest the hill, and feathered the trigger with the silky touch of a butterfly.

The explosion sounded like a cannon going off. The force of the big Sharps slammed into him, rocking Jedidiah backwards. On the distant hill, the Comanchero suddenly arched in the saddle, one hand clawing at the new hole in his back, before slumping sideways from his charging mount. His body bounced like a rag doll as it tumbled along the ground.

For a long moment Jedidiah squatted motionless, his gaze crawling slowly over the battlefield surrounding the partially built cabin. Riderless horses stood or milled about nervously. Lifeless bodies littered the whole area and brought back dark memories of the war: memories of haunting scenes, scenes he tried and failed to forget in the years since. Fighting Comanchero and Indians seemed different; somehow they were less human in some strange way. They weren't like the men he fought and killed in blue uniforms, often no more than mere boys not unlike Jedidiah, dead before they were old enough to shave.

A movement behind him reached his awareness. He swung toward the sound. It was the farmer and his family emerging from the protection of the, soon to be, cabin.

The farmer was an average sized fellow that wore a pair of patched bib overalls, a dungaree work shirt, and a pair of run-over boots that looked like they needed to be thrown away. He carried an old model Henry that looked to be as worn out as his boots. His shock of light brown hair hung shoulder length and framed a clean-shaven face that right now showed a lot of mad.

"You didn't have to shoot those two men in the back!" he near shouted, his voice shaking with anger. "They were riding away! That was nothing but murder."

"Woe there," Jedidiah said, lifting to his feet and biting back a sudden flare of anger. "Just hold on a cotton-picking minute! First off, those were Comanchero that was trying to kill you and your whole family. They were within a few minutes of slitting your throat and doing all kind of unspeakable things to your womenfolk. If I had let those men ride off, they would have been back with a hundred of their compadres to finish what they started.

"I don't know where you're from mister, but out here, there ain't no such thing as fighting fair. If a man's trying to do harm to you or yours, you kill him. That's just the way it is. Front or back, it don't make a lick of difference as long as you get him before he gets you.

"If old Amos Hobbs hadn't asked me to look in on you folks you'd all be dead right now. If you got a lick of sense, you'll load your family in those wagons and move closer to the fort or back where you come from, makes no difference to me. I've had my say. I'll be riding on."

Jedidiah turned and took up his reins and swiveled a stirrup to toe it...then paused. For the first time he noticed the rest of the farmer's family. They stood together not more than twenty feet away and couldn't have kept from hearing every word of his lecture.

Two strapping boys that looked to be fourteen or so were the spitting image of one another—twins. Both had hair that hung near their shoulders and was the color of ripe cornhusk. They had ruddy complexions, blue eyes, and pleasant faces. Both held a rifle loosely in their hands.

The mother was a fine looking woman somewhere on the sundown side of forty. She wore a gingham dress that touched her ankles and heavy men's work shoes. Her prematurely gray-streaked hair was made up into a bun on the back of her head. Her face radiated with a rare, deep beauty that even the tiredness in her blue eyes couldn't hide.

Then he saw her. The last remaining member of the family emerged from behind the log wall and moved to join her mother. Jedidiah's breath caught and his heart stopped beating. She was the most beautiful creature he had ever seen.

Several inches taller than her mother, she looked to be nineteen or so with a grown-up shape, if he was any judge. She wore a flowered skirt beneath a white blouse that hung off her bare shoulders and offered the slightest glimpse of youthful breasts. It was enough to cause a fellow to wonder about the rest.

She moved with the sinuous grace of a mountain lioness, lithe and youthful. Her long, golden hair hung loosely about her shoulders. The early morning sun's crimson rays crowned her head and set it ablaze with shimmering color. A light breeze from somewhere kissed the strands and sent them flying. A curled finger lifted and brushed them aside, revealing a face that would make an angel envious.

Her features were delicate, with high cheekbones and a complexion the color of fresh cream. Her misty-green eyes rose to meet Jedidiah's own, and lingered for a fleeting moment. He thought they were the most provocative eyes he had ever seen.

There was a smoldering sensuality about her, some combination of innocence and earthiness that Jedidiah found strangely captivating. Time ceased. A huge lump crawled up the back of his throat. His heart pounded like an Apache's war drum. His mouth went suddenly dry.

He doffed his hat, both as a gesture of good manners and because his head suddenly needed to breathe.

"Wait..." he vaguely heard the farmer speaking but was unable to concentrate on what was being said.

"What?...uh...what were you saying?" Jedidiah stammered and fiddled with his hat. His gaze never wavered from the real object of his attention.

"I reckon I might have been a tad hasty a minute ago," the farmer said, his eyes watching the toe of his work boots draw lines in the dirt. "The wife says I've got a way of letting my mouth outrun my thinking sometimes. I reckon this was one of those times. It's just...well, the Bible says "Thou shalt not kill."

"Yes, sir," Jedidiah agreed, "but I recall it saying something about turning the other cheek too. I tried that for a while, all it ever got me was two black eyes instead of one. I just wouldn't advise doing that with a Comanchero."

"I'm awfully sorry I flew off the handle like that," the farmer said, extending a hand. "I'll be begging your pardon. I'd like to start over. I'm Wesley Johnson. That is my wife, Adrianna. Those are our twin boys, Denver and Dewey, they're fourteen going on twenty. The one with the pretty smile is our daughter, Julianna."

Jedidiah took the offered hand and felt the strength of the man. His callused, work-hardened hands clasped with Jedidiah's own in a warm handshake.

"I'm Jedidiah Boone," he said, purposefully avoiding the daughter's searching eyes that he could feel appraising him from head to toe. "It's nice to meet you folks."

"If Wesley won't say it, I will," Mrs. Johnson spoke up. "Thank you, Mr. Boone, for saving our family. If you hadn't come along when you did..."

"Yes, of course," Wesley Johnson interrupted. "Thank you, Mr. Boone. No doubt, you risked your life to save us. I must say, I fought in the war, but I've never seen anyone fight like that."

"A man does what he has to do," Jedidiah said.

"Mr. Boone," Mrs. Johnson spoke up again. "Julianna and I were preparing breakfast when we saw those men coming. Would you join us?"

"I...I don't mind if I do, Ma'am, if you have enough. A fellow gets tired of his own cooking on the trail."

"Then have a seat over by the fire and we'll get you men a cup of hot coffee," she said.

"I'll get them a cup, mother," Julianna said, her voice sounding so sweet the birds must have stopped their singing just to listen.

"Boys," Mr. Johnson said, turning to his twin sons. "Why don't you hitch up a team to one of the wagons? We need to load up those men and give them a proper burying. We'll catch up those horses and turn them in the corral with ours. Strip them saddles off, too. While you're at it, gather up all the weapons you can find, they might come in handy later on."

"Where you folks from?" Jedidiah asked as he walked with Wesley Johnson toward one of the covered wagons.

"We had a hardscrabble farm in the boot heel of Missouri. Didn't have enough ground to hardly keep food on the table. We decided to make a fresh start and signed on with a wagon train bound for Colorado. Our two youngest girls took sick and we had to stop. The train went on without us. We buried them right over there under that big oak tree. I told the wife I weren't going no further. I decided to stay right here."

They strode up to the fire and were met by Julianna with two tin cups of steaming coffee. Mr. Johnson took one and folded onto a log near the campfire. Turning, she held out the other cup to Jedidiah. Her eyes lifted slowly. Their gaze met...and held for a long moment. He reached a hand for his cup. The tip of his fingers touched hers. The thrill of that touch shot up his arm and raced straight to his heart.

"Thank...you," he managed to get out in a whisper, trying to shutter the feelings welling up inside him.

The faintest hint of a quick smile curled one corner of her full lips. It was a pretty smile, and he liked the way it looked on her.

"Breakfast will be ready in a few minutes," she said.

Those were the first words she spoke to him. They pleasured him. He decided right then and there that he would remember the sound for the rest of his life.

It was a delicious meal of Dutch oven biscuits, salt pork, and flour gravy. All of the men folk, including Jedidiah, had second helpings.

"I don't recall ever eating a better meal, Mrs. Johnson," Jedidiah said, draining the last sip of coffee from his cup.

"Thank you, Mr. Boone," she said, smiling sweetly and flicking a quick glance at her husband. "A woman always likes to hear that her efforts are appreciated, but I'm afraid most of the credit should go to Julianna. She's a much better cook than I am."

"Well, I'm certain she learned it from you," he said, swinging a quick glance at Julianna as she came toward him.

"Would you like another cup of coffee, Mr. Boone?" she asked, extending a hand to take his cup.

Once again their gaze met and his heart skipped a beat.

She turned on a toe and moved smoothly to the blackened coffeepot sitting on a flat rock near the flames. His gaze watched the wigwag of her hips with an appreciative look and followed as she bent to pour the coffee. The thin material of her blue skirt stretched tight against the fullness of her perfectly shaped hips. His breath caught. She had all the right round places, and a waist so small he would wager he could encircle it with both hands.

Oh Lord, he thought. What am I doing? What's happening to me? I can't keep my eyes off of her.

"That's a strange looking dog," Mr. Johnson said, tilting a head toward the wolf dog lying quietly under one of the wagons. "He looks more like a full-growed wolf than a dog. What's his name?"

"Dog," Jedidiah said simply.

"Shore wouldn't want to meet up with him in the dark."

"I've raised him from a pup."

After breakfast Jedidiah and Mr. Johnson helped the twins bury the Comanchero a half mile from the house behind a grove of dogwood trees. It was a tiring and gruesome task. While they worked, they talked.

"I guess I don't understand, Jedidiah," Wesley said as they rolled another body into a freshly dug grave. "Who are these Comanchero? Where do they live?"

"They're a loose knit band of cold bloodied killers. They're human vultures that prey upon the weak and helpless. They run in gangs like packs of wolves savaging the countryside. Mostly they're white men, but there's lots of Mexicans and Indians that ride with them, too. They're mostly undesirables their own people have rejected and cast out. They trade guns and whiskey with the Indians for white captives and sell them down in Mexico. The women and girls are sold into prostitution and the men are sold as slaves to work the silver mines.

"In this part of the territory they are led by a half-breed they call Scarface. He's a bad one. He's half Apache, half white man, and poison mean. No one knows for shore what he looks like except that he's got a long knife scar from his left eye down to the corner of his mouth. Most that's laid eyes on him are dead.

"They raid all over the territory and even down into Mexico, then skedaddle back to their hideout, but nobody that's been there has ever come back alive. Even the army ain't anxious to tangle with them"

"Mr. Johnson, I've got to be honest with you. You just flat ain't gonna make it out here where you are. Oh sure, this is good, rich farmland. This ground would most likely grow anything a man had a mind to plant. There'll come a time when a man could have a good life in this country. But you're two hundred miles from the nearest army fort. Your nearest neighbor is old Amos Hobbs and he wouldn't be able to help in time of trouble.

"I'm gonna talk straight to you, Mr. Johnson. You've got a nice family but you're gonna get them killed. Just as sure as the sun comes up in the west, you're all gonna die. It might be tonight, it might be in a week or a month, but if you stay here, you're all gonna die. If the Comanchero don't get you the Apaches will."

"But we come all the way from Missouri and the only Indians we saw were friendly. We've been here most of two months now and we ain't seen hide nor hair of an Indian."

"The only time you see an Apache is when he wants you to see him. By then, it's most likely too late. The reason I'm down this way, I'm searching for two white girls. One of them is eleven years old and the other one is seven. About a month ago the Apaches raided their ranch. They cut the throats of six Mexicans that worked on the ranch while they were still in their bunks. Then they broke into the hacienda and cut the father's stomach open and strung his guts all over the room and scalped him while he was still alive.

"Only God knows how many of them raped the mother before they cut off her breasts and slit her throat from ear to ear. They took the two little girls captive. I don't know what they got in mind to do with them but I've got to try and get them back.

"Now, if that's what you're willing to let happen to your family, you just stay here and I'll promise you that's exactly what's gonna happen."

Wesley Johnson was a shaken man. Sweat beaded on his forehead. His face was chalky-white. For a long space of time he just stood silently with his head down, leaning on his shovel.

"But what can I do, Jedidiah?" he finally asked pitifully. "Everything we've got in the world is in those two wagons. I wanted to start a new life for the wife and kids. I wanted them to have a little piece of ground where we could make a living and be happy.

"We can't make it to Colorado by ourselves. You're telling me we can't stay here. What choice do I have?"

"Mr. Johnson, the way I see it you got three choices. You can stay here and get your family killed. You can go with me as far as Fort Bowie down near Apache Pass and maybe find a piece of ground near the fort. Or..."

"Or what?"

"Or, I could show you a place I know that's about the prettiest little valley you ever laid eyes on. It's called, Angel FireValley. There's a waterfall and an ice-cold mountain stream where the trout jump clear out of the water. The ground is black bottomland so rich and fertile a man would have to start harvesting might near before he got through planting. There's timber for building and good grass for fattening livestock. It's a place where a man could build a home, raise a family, and carve out a good life for his children and his children's children. I know, I live there. It's the closest thing to heaven I've found on earth."

"You saying the land's for the taking?" the man asked, excitement creeping into his voice.

"It's yours if you want it."

"Are you saying you'll take us there?" Johnson asked.

"Well, like I say, I've got to do my best to find those girls, but if you could backtrack as far as Sante Fe, I'll have someone guide you to the valley."

"Mr. Boone, I'll talk to the wife, but I already know what she'll say. I'd say you just got yourself a neighbor."

"Good. Now lets get the rest of these fellows planted and start packing those wagons. I'll ride with you as far as Hobbs Station. If we get started by noon, we can make it be this time tomorrow."

Chapter Four

The wagons were packed and ready to roll. The bulky workhorses stood hipshot in their harnesses, swishing away annoying horseflies with their long tails. The seven Comanchero horses, the milk cows and the bull were all tied on long lead ropes to the back of the wagons.

Julianna and the twins had already spent time under the big oak tree saying their good-byes to their two younger sisters. Now Wesley and Adrianna Johnson headed that way, walking slowly, their hands intertwined.

Jedidiah sat his saddle and watched, as they stood motionless and silent for long moments beside the two small mounds of dirt. Kneeling, Mrs. Johnson slowly reached a hand and placed a small bouquet of wild flowers on each of the graves. She lifted a hand to wipe away tears, then rose, turned her back, and walked away sobbing.

Jedidiah's heart tugged at his chest at the heartbreaking scene. He swallowed a big lump that crawled up his throat and threatened to choke him. They are leaving behind part of themselves, he thought. They will never be completely whole again.

The twins drove the wagons. Mrs. Johnson sat beside the boy named Dewey. Jedidiah had learned to tell him from his brother because Denver was left-handed. Wesley Johnson had chosen one of the Comanchero horses, a big black gelding, as his own and volunteered to ride drag to watch their back trail.

Julianna rode another of the newly acquired horses, a blood-red bay mare with a blaze face and four white stockings. She had changed clothes and now wore a pair of men's pants and a beige blouse that buttoned up the front. Both fit her really good, Jedidiah thought. The pants offered only the slightest hint that all of his speculations had been right. She had long and shapely legs. The well-filled blouse set his imagination racing anew.

Jedidiah took the lead as the little procession pulled out. They hadn't gone far before Julianna reined the mare up beside him. The nearness of her caused goose bumps to pop out and tingle his skin. His eyes kept betraying him and strayed again and again to sights he shouldn't be gazing at.

"Will we get to the trading post tonight?" she asked, riding stirrup to stirrup with him.

"No," he replied, forcing his gaze away from where it wanted to dwell. "We'll find a place to camp tonight and get there before noon tomorrow."

"Mother says we are going to the place where you live. She called it Angel Fire Valley. That's a beautiful name."

"It's a beautiful place," he told her. "I reckon it's about the most beautiful valley I've ever seen."

"Do you live there?"

"My cabin is on Angel Fire Mountain that overlooks the waterfall and the valley. I live there with a black couple that's been with my family since before I was born."

"Is there...is there a Mrs. Boone?"

"No," he said, for some reason feeling somewhat embarrassed at the question. "I reckon I've never found anybody that could put up with me."

"I find that hard to believe," she said, turning her gaze to settle full on his face.

Unable to find the power to control his eyes, they found hers...and their gaze lingered for what seemed like an eternity.

"So, let me see if I understand," she said, still searching his face with her eyes. The hint of a mischievous smile lifted one corner of her lips. "You have a dog named Dog, a mule you call Mule, a horse named Butternut, and you live with a black couple on a mountain called Angel Fire? You're a most unusual man, Mr. Boone."

"Yes, ma'am, I reckon I am," he told her, the trace of a smile tugging at his lips. "More than a few have told me that. I am who I am and don't pretend to be something I ain't."

"That's an admirable trait. I'll make an agreement with you, Mr. Boone. If you'll stop calling me ma'am, I'll stop calling you, Mr. Boone. Agreed?"

"Then what should I call you?" he asked.

"My name is Julianna."

"Julianna," he repeated, feeling the pleasure of the sound rolling across his tongue. "That's a beautiful name for a..." suddenly realizing what he was about to say, his voice trailed off.

"Thank you, Jedidiah, for the compliment you almost gave me," she said, a happy little laugh escaping her lips.

They again rode in silence for a ways. The afternoon sun beat down relentlessly. Jedidiah swiped his gray Stetson from his head and sleeved sweat from his forehead as he peered ahead.

"When we get to the trading post you will leave us?" she asked, her voice betraying the feeling behind the question.

"Yes," he answered, wishing he didn't have to say the word. "I have to try my best to find those little girls."

"When will you...?" she asked, her voice trailing off.

Jedidiah fumbled to find an answer and had to swallow before he could give it.

"I don't know," he told her honestly.

For a long time they rode in silence, each lost in their own thoughts, each framing a hundred questions neither knew how to ask.

Jedidiah noticed Julianna's mare favoring its left foreleg.

"Rein up a minute," he told her. "Your horse is limping. I want to check its hoof."

He stepped down and lifted the mare's hoof. After a moment's examination, he withdrew the Bowie from his belt scabbard and used the point to flick a small pebble from the horse's hoof. Remounting, they rode on toward a stand of paloverde trees.

"Oh look!" she shouted excitedly as a doe burst from a grove of scrub oak up ahead followed closely by a young fawn. They bounded off in high leaps toward the safety of a deeper stand of trees.

Jedidiah glanced only quickly at the fleeing deer. He was captured by the flush of excitement that filled Julianna's beautiful face. Her eyes sparkled and danced. For the briefest instant she was a little girl again, filled with all the innocence and recklessness of childhood.

A fresh running creek, green grass for good graze for the stock, and a little clearing in a grove of sycamore trees convinced Jedidiah it would be a good place to camp for the night. There was still a good hour of sun but he was afraid they might not find another spot before dark.

Without being told, everyone pitched in to set up camp and take care of the chores that needed done. The men folk pitched in and got a fire going. They cut and stacked wood nearby for the next morning's breakfast fire and knowing the nights could get surprisingly chilly. Julianna fetched water from the stream and put on a pot of coffee while Mrs. Johnson began preparing supper.

The twins milked the two cows to relieve their heavy bags and to supply milk for cooking and to churn for butter. Jedidiah and Wesley tended to the stock, unsaddling, watering, and hobbling them so they could graze the fetlock-high grass.

Supper was a joyous affair. They dined on deer stew, hot Dutch oven biscuits, and fried apple pies. There was an air of excitement. Laughter came easy and often. Jedidiah found himself caught up in the family atmosphere, the first he had experienced in a mighty long time. He liked the feeling.

After supper they sipped coffee around the campfire and visited. The fire crackled loudly and spat friendly orange tongues of flame into the night. There were many excited questions about the valley they were headed for. As he told them about the Angel Fire Valley he saw Mr. and Mrs. Johnson flicking happy glances between each other.

"It just sounds too good to be true," Adrianna Johnson said, excitement showing clearly on her face. "The mountain you live on sounds like a beautiful place."

"Yes ma'am," Jedidiah said. "I reckon a mountain is a lot like a man. Up close, it looks like just a big pile of rocks. Sometimes you have to step back and look at the whole thing before you realize the horizon is changed by it."

"We'll want to build us a cabin first thing," Mr. Johnson announced. "We ought to be able to get it done before winter sets in."

"There's timber aplenty and rock for a fireplace," Jedidiah assured him, "all close by. I'll send word and ask Mose to give you a hand. He's got a knack for building. Me and him built my place up on the mountain."

"How much clearing will we have to do before we can plant a crop in the spring?" Wesley inquired.

"There's cleared and open ground in the valley just waiting to be plowed and planted. The ground's rich and well watered from mountain runoff."

"Wesley, I'll need a big place for a garden, too" Mrs. Johnson said, hardly able to contain her excitement.

"I reckon we could find time to break you up a spot," her husband assured her, flicking her a secret smile.

"Mr. Jedidiah," the twin named Dewey spoke up. "You say there's fish in that river, too?"

"They might near jump right out on the bank at a fellow," Jedidiah joshed the boy.

"Boy-oh-boy," the boy exclaimed, his youthful face splitting in a nutcracker grin. "I'm gonna like this place."

"I reckon as how we all are," Wesley Johnson agreed.

"Think I'll stroll down and take a gander at that mare's foot where I took that rock out this afternoon," Jedidiah said, pushing to his feet. "Wouldn't want her to go lame on you."

"I'll walk with you," Julianna spoke up quickly.

A small smile tugged at the corner of his mouth and his heart raced.

It took only a few minutes to confirm what Jedidiah already knew; the mare's foot was fine. Afterwards, the quiet night beckoned and it seemed only natural for them to stroll down beside the creek. They stopped on the bank and stared silently at the water.

A gentle evening breeze whispered softly through the leaves. A full moon sifted through the sycamore trees and dappled the water's surface with shimmering patterns of light.

"It's a Comanche moon," Jedidiah said absently.

"What's that?"

"It's what the Indians call a full moon. Legend has it the only time they will fight at night is when the moon is full. They believe that if they are killed at night their spirit will wander in darkness forever, unable to find its way to the happy hunting ground. That's what they call their heaven."

"That's a beautiful legend. Is it true?"

"I can't rightly say. I've never fought the Comanche. One thing for shore, the Apache hold no beliefs like that. They'll kill you day or night, makes no difference to them."

"Why do they want to kill us? We haven't harmed them."

"That's not the way they see it. They look on us as intruders. This is their land. Their ancestors were here hundreds, maybe even thousands, of years before we showed up. Look at it this way.

Suppose after your folks get to Angel Fire Valley and you work hard to cut down trees and build a nice home, you plow the ground and plant a crop. Then all of a sudden somebody else shows up and decides they want what's yours. How would you feel about it?"

"I see what you mean. It don't seem quite fair does it?"

"Not hardly."

They listened to the night birds and gazed up at the stars.

"The sky seems somehow larger here than it did back in Missouri," she said.

"Yeah," Jedidiah sighed. "It sorta makes one mindful of his insignificance, don't it?"

"I used to sit for hours and look at the night sky." Julianna said, her voice hardly louder than a whisper. "I believe God made the stars for lovers. Why else would He have put them there?"

He knuckled his wheat-colored mustache for a long moment.

"Maybe He just wanted to light up the sky," Jedidiah joshed her, a wry smile hitching up one corner of his mouth.

His kidding earned him a playful swat on his shoulder with a dainty hand.

"Do you have to go?" she asked hesitantly...almost pleadingly.

"Yes, but I'll be back before you know it. You won't hardly have time to miss me."

"I miss you already."

A long, comfortable silence followed as they enjoyed the night, and each other's presence. Jedidiah could somehow feel her eyes upon him. He swung a glance. Their gazes met, their hearts in their eyes, and seemed to speak a language all their own. They spoke of questions without answers. They spoke of feelings that mere words could not express. They spoke of promises that could not be asked nor given.

"Julianna...I..." Reason refused to allow him to speak the words his heart was screaming out to be said. He couldn't. He shouldn't, at least not now, not yet, and maybe not ever. He must shutter his feelings deep inside. He had given Mr. Fargo his word that he would do his best to find the kidnapped girls. A man's word was his bond; he would die if need be before he would break that promise. A soft silence closed around his words and he tore his gaze away, staring off into the distance at the twinkling stars.

The sun was near noon when they forded the Rio Grande River and the wagons lumbered to a stop in front of Hobb's trading post. Trace chains rattled. Wagon horses snorted and blew great bursts of air through their muzzles exhausted from tugging the two heavy wagons up the steep riverbank.

Jedidiah reined up as Amos Hobbs strode toward them with that old double-barrel shotgun cradled in the crook of his arm. Wesley Johnson pulled his horse to a stop nearby, his rifle lay across the front of his saddle.

"Howdy Jedidiah. See ye ran into the farmer and his family," the trapper said, sweeping an eye over the Comanchero horses tied on leads behind the wagons. "Appears you folks come by some extra horses somewhere along the way."

"Yep," Jedidiah said, swinging a leg over his saddle and stepping to the ground.

"Them ain't Apache ponies. Looks more like Comanchero. You folks have trouble?"

"Some. Don't guess you heard anything about those two girls?"

"Not a word. Howdy to you, Mr. Johnson," Hobbs said, spitting a long stream of tobacco juice at the ground. "You folks decide to head back to where you come from?"

"Mr. Boone told us about a valley near where he lives. We're headed there."

"You don't say? Now that's right neighborly of you, Jedidiah. Never knowed you was the sociable sort."

"Most likely a whole lot about me you don't know, Amos."

"Mr. Boone happened along just at the right time," Wesley Johnson said. "We were under attack by the Comanchero. He probably saved all our lives."

Amos Hobbs flicked a concerned look at Jedidiah.

"You get 'em all?"

"Yep."

The hint of a smile parted the trader's whiskered face.

"You got some paper and ink?" Jedidiah asked. "I need to write a couple of notes before these folks move on. They're wanting to make some tracks before dark."

"I expect I can find some somewhere," Hobbs said. "You folks light down and rest the teams. You're welcome to spend a day or two if'n you're a mind."

"Thanks," Johnson said, "but we're anxious to get to that valley Mr. Boone told us about."

"I expect so," Amos Hobbs said, aiming another grin at Jedidiah. "Come on. I'll rustle up that paper for you."

While the Johnsons stretched their legs and rested the horses, Jedidiah scribbled two quick notes and folded the papers in half. He strode out to where Wesley Johnson was adjusting the linkage of the trace chains. He handed the farmer one of the notes.

"When you get to Sante Fe, go to the Wells Fargo office. Give this note to a man by the name of Winston Taylor, he's a friend of mine. He'll arrange for a stock of supplies that we'll all need to make it through the winter. It'll save us a long trip into Taos later on. He'll also send someone with you to lead you folks to the Angel Fire Valley.

"When you get to the valley, give this other note to Mose. He's the big black man I told you about that lives with me. Him and his wife, Minnie, are like family. They'll help you folks build your cabin and get settled."

"How will I find him?"

"Don't worry about finding him, he'll find you. There ain't nothing goes on in the valley he don't know about."

"When will you be coming back?"

"When I can," Jedidiah said, looping Butternut's reins over his neck and toeing a stirrup.

"Thanks, Jedidiah, for all your help."

"Keep a sharp eye between here and Sante Fe. Ride with your guns handy. Don't care how friendly they appear, don't let 'em get close, understand?"

"We'll be careful. You do the same."

Jedidiah swung a glance at Amos Hobbs and his squaw standing near the front door of the trading post. A quick lift of his head was his goodbye.

"Keep your hat pulled low over that gold hair of yours," the trapper said, spitting a mouthful of tobacco juice. "Shore hate to spot it on some Apache's belt one of these days."

"Me, too," Jedidiah said, reining his horse around.

Julianna sat quietly on her red mare in the shade of a big sycamore tree not far from the wagons. She had watched as Jedidiah talked with her father. Dread of the upcoming goodbye coiled inside her, twisting and writhing like a snake. She trembled in terrible anticipation.

I don't want to say goodbye. She thought.

For the first time in her life she had met someone she was attracted to. His mere nearness had given birth to yearnings in her she had never known before. Yearnings she had never imagined she could feel. It was like a door had suddenly swung open, giving her the briefest glimpse of a future, of a husband, of children, of a home. Now she was about to say goodbye.

Drawing a long, shaky breath, she tried to quell the flood of regret that washed over her. Her heart thundered beneath her ribs.

She aimed her gaze at the ground as he slowly walked his horse toward her. She must not allow him to look into her eyes, he would surely see right into the depths of her very soul.

He reined up beside her. Her face flushed. Her chest filled. A sob squirmed its way up the back of her throat. She bit back tears that threatened to flood her eyes.

"No good-byes," he whispered.

Her throat was too full to speak. Not trusting her voice, Julianna only nodded.

For a moment he hesitated, as if waiting ...for something. Then he reined around and nudged his pinto...and slowly rode away.

I can't! Her heart screamed out. I can't let him ride away without saying goodbye! I might never see him again!

She had to clear her throat twice before his name worked its way past the knot on a quivering sob.

"Jedidiah," she choked out.

Twisting a quick look over his shoulder, his lips lifted in a smile that occupied most of his face. Reining the pinto around, he was at her side. Leaning over, a strong arm swept her from her saddle into his arms. Her gaze found his and discovered her own yearning mirrored in his sky-blue eyes. They were the bluest eyes she had ever seen, like two deep, dark pools beneath a summer sky. Her head reeled. Her heartbeat flickered and picked up speed.

His knuckles lightly grazed her cheek, tender, caressing, and with that simple touch, an unfamiliar longing rose full and hot in her chest. It spilled through her, slow and honey sweet. Julianna's breath caught in her throat. A low moan erupted from deep inside her.

His lips breached the slight distance between them. He kissed her with a sweet, simmering intensity that made her head whirl and sent delight surging over her body. Deep within the secret heart of her, tinder of desire was ignited. Goose-bumps pricked her skin as some strange, wild, indefinable emotion she had never felt before tingled down her spine, frightening her, exciting her, bewildering her. She was trembling and feverish when he raised his mouth from hers. He was the first man that ever kissed her.

He lifted her back into her saddle with a soft sigh.

"I'll be back," he whispered, his eyes echoing his promise.

Their hands parted by degrees, fingers trailing apart slowly until only their fingertips touched. He nudged his horse forward and looked away. She watched through tear- puddled eyes until he disappeared into the distance. He never once looked back.

Rebecca had cried herself to sleep again. She had been doing that more and more lately. Elizabeth was worried about her sister. She couldn't get her to eat. She hardly said a word anymore. She just sat and stared at the wall...and cried.

Elizabeth idly picked up the sharp stone. As she had done each day since shortly after their arrival, she made another scratch mark in the adobe wall. Thirty-two. She counted thirty-two marks.

What would become of them? Why were they keeping them locked up here? Should they try to escape and run away? How could they possibly escape? Where would they go? She didn't even know where they were. Maybe she could talk Two Deers Running into helping them escape—not much chance of that. The questions swirled through her mind. She was confused, frightened.

She sat on the floor in front of the only door to the one-room shack. Her face was pressed to the crack in the heavy plank door. Lately, while Rebecca slept, she had spent hours each day peeking through the small opening, watching the comings and goings of the Comanchero camp.

She had learned from Two Deers Running the ugly Indian that had taken them from their home and killed her parents was called Nantaje. Elizabeth counted seven other Indians that usually rode in and out of camp with him. They would leave, then in two or three days, they would return. Sometimes leading stolen horses, sometimes with packhorses loaded down with all kinds of stuff.

She estimated at least another twenty men in the camp besides the Indians. Most looked like Mexicans, but a few were white men. She noticed about half of them had ridden out a few days before and still hadn't returned.

It was plain the one called Scarface, was the leader. He lived with a beautiful young Mexican girl, not many years older than herself, in an adobe shack on the far side of the river. He rode a beautiful solid black horse and would disappear for two or three days at a time.

Several days ago she had been watching from her peephole when an argument broke out between Scarface and one of the Mexicans. Without any warning a long knife had magically appeared in his hand and in the blink of an eye, he had killed the man, stabbing him several times. Afterward, he had calmly wiped the blood from his knife on the man's shirt and walked away. She hadn't slept good since then. She kept having nightmares about the brutal killing.

Yesterday she had seen three men ride into camp. Her heart leaped inside her chest because they were all three well-dressed white men. They didn't look like any of the others that usually rode in and out of the camp. One of them rode a pretty black and white pinto. The other two wore funny looking little black hats. Maybe they're coming to get us to take us home, she thought.

A careful flutter of hope unfurled inside her mind. A feeling of excitement swelled. Her heart pounded. Should she wake Rebecca and tell her? No, she decided. I better wait until I'm sure. No use getting her hopes up for nothing.

She watched anxiously as the one called Scarface walked from one of the huts to meet them. They had talked for a few minutes. The leader had pointed toward the hut where she and her sister was being held. Scarface and the little fat man started up the hill. Elizabeth quickly scooted away from the door, crawling over to sit beside her sister.

The door swung open. Scarface stepped inside followed closely by the man in the business suit. He looked nervous. He had taken one quick look at them, then turned quickly and hurried out the door.

After she heard the bar being put in place on the door, she crawled quickly over to her crack and watched as all three men mounted and rode away. Afterward, she had cried herself to sleep.

Today as she watched, the sound of horses reached her ears. She leaned to the side to see what it was. Six big, heavily armed Mexicans galloped into camp. Like the others, their clothes were filthy. Their faces masked by heavy beards. Leather bandoleers criss-crossed their chests. Large sombreros hung down their backs, suspended by neck cords. Two girls lay face down across the saddles in front of two of the riders, their long hair hanging down and flying in the wind. Elizabeth caught her breath in a gasp of air. More captives!

As she watched breathlessly, the riders reined to a stop in the center of the jumble of adobe huts. Scarface himself strode from one of the buildings to meet his men. The two girls were dumped unceremoniously onto the ground. Everyone laughed loudly.

Scarface took a step to stand over them. Reaching down, he grabbed a handful of hair of the nearest one and yanked her head up. For a long moment he stared at her. The girl was Mexican. From what Elizabeth could see, she looked to be no more than fourteen. His other hand grasped the cotton blouse the girl wore and ripped it from her, leaving her naked from the waist up. Using the same process, he inspected the second girl, who looked to be the older of the two.

With a wave of his hand, he selected two of the riders that had brought the girls in. With a happy yell, they jumped from their horses and each grabbed one of the girls, half dragging the screaming girls toward one of the nearby huts.

Lying on her blanket that night beside Rebecca, Elizabeth couldn't sleep. Hot tears brimmed her eyelids and scorched trails down her cheeks. She didn't even bother to wipe them away. Her mind was filled with the imagined horrors of what the two girls must be going through. Would the girls be killed? Why were they being treated differently than her and Rebecca? Would they soon be taken to those huts by one of those men? Her body shook with the cold chills that surged over her at the thought. Lying in the darkness she balled the wool blanket against her mouth to muffle her sobs, her body shook with spasms of hopelessness.

Chapter Five

It had been a week since he left Hobbs Station. What had appeared only as a dark outline against the western sky two days ago, now loomed over him, lifting their lofty peaks upward until it seemed they would punch holes in the sky. High above, the mountains compressed the sky to a narrow patch of soft blue.

He was now entering the Pyramid Mountain range. It would be tough riding, but much shorter than following the old Butterfield stage route that swung far to the south. Tomorrow he would cross the Continental Divide. Another two days across the Sonoran Desert should bring him to the Apache Pass and Fort Bowie. He had decided to rest there a couple of days and see what information he could pick up about Cochise.

The country had changed steadily. Leaving the rolling foothills behind him, he now rode through heavy forest interrupted by hulking gray rocks that shouldered close to the narrow trail. Great boulders protruded from the earth like gigantic monuments. Giant trees stood sentry, majestic, pointing their long fingers toward the clouds. Even the stream the trail followed and which he forded, and forded again, had to fight its way along the rock-strewn bed carved from the mountain over bygone centuries. The angry whitewater rushed down from the mountains and tumbled over large boulders along streambeds, emitting a constant roar, and reminded Jedidiah of Angel Fire Falls...and home.

At mid afternoon he struck a road of sorts. Fairly recent wagon tracks told him it would lead him through the mountains. He lengthened the lead rope on Mule.

"Come on, Dog," he spoke to his companion trotting along beside his pinto. "We'll sleep high on the mountain tonight."

Near the mountain pass, the beginning of a small mountain stream doglegged sharply to avoid a sheer, thirty foot cliff face and left a small, grassy clearing peppered with a scattering of large cedar and pine trees. He figured it would be a good place to camp for the night.

After unsaddling and watering his horse and pack mule, he hobbled them on good graze and set out to find his supper. He hadn't walked fifty yards before spotting a big fox squirrel scampering up a tree toward its nest. A single shot to the head from thirty yards brought it tumbling from the tall pine.

In minutes, he had a fire going, coffee boiling, and the dressed squirrel on a wood spike hanging over the leaping flames.

"No need of you eyeing it," he told the wolf dog, who was lying nearby with his muzzle resting on his paws. "That's my supper. You'll have to find your own."

As if the big dog understood, he pushed to his feet and trotted off into the woods.

After supper, Jedidiah leaned back against his saddle and sipped steaming coffee from a tin cup. It was a clear night. A thin slice of silver moon peeked above a mountain peak and climbed slowly into the sky. It bathed the little clearing and surrounding area in shades of indigo and black. The tall pine trees cast long shadows. The velvety, black canopy overhead was littered with a myriad of twinkling diamond stars that seemed so close he could almost reach out and touch them. He sipped his coffee and listened to the night sounds: the musical rustle of water over rocks, the lonesome call of a whippoorwill, the constant drone of crickets. Somewhere an owl asked the eternal question, and a coyote barked into the night. He slowly knuckled his beard then tugged at his ear in thoughtful contemplation.

Wonder where Julianna and her family are? They should have made it to Sante Fe a couple of days ago.

The mere thought of her brought a warm feeling to his chest and a smile to his lips. He had never met anyone like her. It was like she had cast some sort of spell over him: The way she looked at him with those dancing eyes, the way she moved, the sound of her voice. When they touched, a surge of energy coursed from his fingers, up his arm, and straight to his heart. No doubt about it, he was smitten by her. He knew in his heart what he felt for her was strong enough to last a lifetime. He wished he were with her this very minute. But he had a job to do.

He harbored no illusions about his chances for success in that regard. Even if he could find Cochise and his men, which wasn't likely, the chances of those two little girls still being alive were mighty slim, and his chances of getting out of this alive were slimmer still. But there was no turning back. He had to try.

The slightest hint of sound reached Jedidiah's ears and scattered his thoughts. His body tensed. His senses keened. Slowly, he set the tin coffee cup on the ground beside him and silently lifted the Stevens sawed-off. He peered into the inky darkness in the direction the sound came from.

Dog emerged from the shadows and trotted into the jagged circle of light.

"You're gonna have to learn to bark or something," he complained out loud. "One of these times I'm liable to shoot you."

The wolf dog trotted to his side, waiting for the familiar pat. Jedidiah ruffled the thick coat of blackish fur.

"Guess we're both full as a fat dog tick. We best get some shut-eye. First light will come early up this high."

There was a chill in the air. Jedidiah propped another log on the fire and crawled into his bedroll. Dog curled up beside him. The velvety night wrapped around him.

From the recess of his memory he took out the picture of Julianna standing there on the bank of that little creek, the moonlight setting her golden hair aflame, stars dancing in her eyes. Lordy, Lordy, that memory is enough to keep a man warm on a chilly night. With that picture clutched close, he drifted into a dreamless sleep.

Julianna lay in her bed in the Grand Hotel in Sante Fe. It was the first time she had ever stayed in a hotel. When they arrived late that afternoon, Mr. Taylor, Jedidiah's friend with the Wells Fargo Agency, had arranged for three separate rooms for their family. They would be leaving day after tomorrow when the supplies were loaded in the wagons.

It was a sultry night. A hot, dry wind wafted through the open window of her second story room and fluttered the faded lacy curtain, but offered little relief. The dissonant music of a badly tuned and poorly played rinky-tink piano disturbed the night. Joined with a woman's raucous, throaty laughter from the saloon across the street, it mingled with the creak and clang of passing wagons and men's boisterous voices from the street below.

The thin nightgown was her only night clothing and clung uncomfortably to her perspiring body. Hooking a thumb and finger in the neck, she fanned it up and down. She enjoyed being alone in the room. Growing up, there had been little or no privacy in their tiny, two rooms and a loft shack in the boot heel of Missouri. All five children slept in the cramped loft.

Their farm had been six miles from the nearest town, if you could call it that. Poplar Bluff boasted a General Store, a livery and blacksmith shop, a Methodist church, and two saloons. School was held in the church. She drove the wagon or rode a horse every day of her eight years schooling.

Not one of the half dozen boys she had gone to school with had interested her; none of them had the sense God gave a goose. After finishing school when she was fifteen, she had ventured into town only on Sunday for church, or on the rare occasion when the church had a picnic or pie supper. The past year she had helped Mrs. Solesbee, the schoolteacher, with the younger kids.

The day her father suggested they sell their small farm and join a wagon train to Colorado had been the happiest day of her life. In Missouri, she had no hope for a life. All she could see in her future were long days of back breaking work only to end up tired and worn out at an early age like her mother, or an old maid school teacher like Mrs. Solesbee. At nineteen, Julianna wanted more out of life than that.

The days and nights on the wagon train had been an exciting adventure. It was something of a shock to discover the whole country wasn't as flat as the Missouri boot heel. She could hardly wait to rise each morning, wondering what wondrous sights awaited her, knowing that each turn of the wagon wheel took them that much closer to the fairy tale country known as Colorado.

Any hopes she harbored for a better life disappeared when Joanna and Jessica took sick. The wagon train had waited for two weeks. From the whispered conversations among the women of the train, it was clear they were getting restless.

She remembered with bitterness the day the wagon master Joshua Kitchens came to their wagon.

"Mr. Johnson," he had said, fidgeting and clearly uncomfortable. "I'm shore sorry about your girl's illness."

"Thank you," her father had said, but it was apparent there was more to be said.

"This is difficult, Mr. Johnson, but you've got to understand our position."

"Your position?"

"We've waited more'n two weeks to see if your girls were gonna get better. We just can't wait no more. We've got to get over the mountains before the snow sets in. We're pulling out in the morning."

"What are you talking about?" her father had asked. "You saying you're leaving without us? You can't do that!"

"I'm afraid we've got to. We just can't wait no longer. I'm sorry."

No one bothered to say goodbye. Julianna and her family had stood together beside their wagons and watched until the wagon train disappeared into the distance. She could still taste the bitter bile of hatred every time she remembered. How could they have done it? How could they have left them there like that?

A week later Joanna and Jessica died.

When her father announced they were establishing their new home where her sisters were buried, Julianna's hopes came crashing down like the end of her world.

Then Jedidiah rode into her life. Unlike the knight in shining armor riding a white charger she had read about in King Arthur's Court, her knight wore buckskins and rode a pinto named Butternut, but he was everything she had ever dreamed about, and more.

It was raining in the mountains. A cold, persistent drizzle wrapped the world in a gloomy haze. A thick fog shrouded the towering peaks and settled across the little clearing where Jedidiah was camped. Now and then, in the faraway mountains, a crooked fork of lightening stabbed the earth, and thunder rumbled a low, ominous warning. It was fixing to storm.

As the first hint of grayness crept over the mountain peaks, Jedidiah awoke from the shallow mist of half sleep. Crawling from his blankets, he coaxed the fire to life and set the leftover coffee from last night over the flames.

Think I'll make do with a cup of coffee for breakfast, he decided.

While the coffee was heating, he led Butternut and Mule down to the stream and watered them. After they had drunk their fill, he saddled the pinto and loaded the packsaddle on Mule. He rolled up his bedroll in the ground sheet and untied his yellow rain poncho from behind his saddle and shrugged into it.

He waited until little whiffs of steam puffed from the spout of the blackened coffeepot before pouring a tin cup full and squatting underneath a low-hanging cedar limb. He blew the steam from his coffee and tested a sip. It burned his tongue but warmed his insides all the way to the pit of his stomach.

Dog trotted over to lie beside him. Jedidiah scratched the dog's ears.

"Shore looking like a soggy trip today," he told his traveling friend, "but best enjoy it while we can, we've still got a desert to cross."

It was one of those quiet moments. One of those times that seals forever the bond between a man and his dog. It was a good time.

Draining the last swallow from his cup, Jedidiah packed the coffeepot away and threaded a stirrup with his boot. Settling into the saddle, he pulled his gray Stetson low, did a half hitch around his saddle horn with Mule's lead, and heeled the pinto into a walk.

They climbed until mid morning, then topped out. Looking down, he saw nothing but a flat layer of gray clouds with an occasional mountain peak poking through. They were above the clouds, an unbelievable sight. They had crossed the Continental Divide. It was said a single drop of rain that fell on this side of the mountain would join countless others and eventually flow into the Pacific Ocean rather than the Atlantic. He found that remarkable.

* * *

By mid afternoon he left the mountains behind and entered a vast wasteland called the Sonoran Desert. It stretched, in seemingly endless flatness, as far as the eye could see, its surface scarred by deep arroyos and wind washed rocks. Gnarled mesquite, greasewood, and crucifixion thorn clung to the white-hot sand and sapped what little moisture the desert could afford to give.

Jedidiah's lungs burned with every breath. The heavy-hanging sun cooked into man and beast, bleeding their strength. There was no relief. There was only the desert: ahead, and behind, and to either side. Sweat ran down his back in small rivulets, blotting through his buckskin shirt and pants and trickled down his legs into his boots. Still he pushed onward.

Panting, Dog pushed ahead half a hundred yards at Jedidiah's signal. Though it would appear they were the only living sojourners in this no man's land, Jedidiah knew from experience the Apache were masters at desert warfare; they knew how to blend into the landscape and move quickly on foot and kill in deadly silence. Just because one didn't see an Apache didn't mean there weren't a dozen within twenty yards of you. He was in Apache territory; he must stay alert.

The wolf dog's big head swiveled from side-to-side, inspecting every arroyo, behind every bush. Alert for any movement, any scent, any sound. A long tailed lizard scampered across his path and disappeared behind a clump of flowering candlewood. A desert owl left his perch on top of a tall barrel cactus and sought the safety of a clump of Joshua trees. Though the desert would appear lifeless, in fact, it teemed with life.

The brilliant red sun approached the distant line of hazy-blue mountains slowly, timidly, like a lover about to say a final goodbye. It gently kissed the lofty peaks one last time before dying for the day and being buried somewhere in the depth of the western horizon.

Behind it, in one last hurrah, as if in a final legacy, it splashed the soft blue sky ablaze with shades of boiling reds, yellows, oranges, and gold that could have come only from God's own paint brush. Streaks of light shot across the sky as if from some great, unseen cannon, careened off the handful of puffy white clouds, framing them with shiny silver. Jedidiah watched, and marveled at God's handiwork.

It would be a dry camp this night. The next water was the spring at Apache Pass.

He slept fitfully, mostly watching the thumbnail moon creep slowly across a star-studded sky. When the Big Dipper told him it was still another three hours until daylight, he rose, saddled up, and made tracks.

By mid morning he approached the Apache Pass, which was nothing more than an opening in a long line of five-thousand foot mountains. If one wanted get to the other side on his way to California, he either went through the pass or rode fifty miles around.

The real draw to Apache Pass, however, was not the pass itself but Apache Spring, a dependable source of fresh water that bubbled out of the ground in a seemingly endless supply. It was the only water source within fifty miles. It had been a few years but Jedidiah knew the area, having scouted it for the army.

Part of some twenty nine million acres, this vast wasteland had been purchased from Mexico in 1854 in what was called the Gadsden Purchase. A military road was built through the pass in 1856 connecting Fort Thorn with Fort Yuma, California. A couple of years later the Butterfield stage line built a stage station beside the all important Apache Springs. The Butterfield line, and it's 141 stage stations, including the one at Apache Pass, had been bought out just two years ago, in 1866, and was now part of the Wells Fargo Agency.

In 1862 the army had built Fort Bowie in the Pass to head off Confederate advances and to stop the ambushes of wagon trains that passed through on their way to California. The Pass was a favorite spot for the Apache to lay in wait, and many unsuspecting travelers had lost their lives here. He had heard a new and larger fort was now under construction.

Riding through thickening groves of mesquite, creosote, and desert willow trees, Jedidiah's animals smelled the spring before they could see it. Dog was the first to scent water and broke into a run. Butternut and Mule smelled it a moment later and picked up their pace. The spring simply bubbled out from underneath some rocks and formed a large pool of cold, clear, sweet tasting water.

Stepping down, Jedidiah loosened the cinch straps on both his mounts so they could slake their thirst. Swiping off his hat, he buried his face in the cold water and drank his fill. Then, filling all four of his empty canteens, he pulled his animals away from the water, knowing too much, too fast, would founder them.

Fort Bowie was undergoing a dramatic change. The old fort had been abandoned. A new, sprawling fort was near completion at a site only a few hundred yards from the original. The new fort was built of adobe and situated on top of a low hill.

To get there, the road passed the cemetery. Scores of headstones, markers, and simple upright stones in the ground stood as silent witnesses of both soldiers and civilians who had died in the pass.

The fort was a beehive of activity. Jedidiah lifted a curled finger to the brim of his hat to acknowledge the greeting of the guard on the front gate. He rode past the laundry, the ordinance building, and the enlisted men's barracks before reining up at the stables.

A young private with a baby face, and horse manure on his black boots, emerged from the stable to meet him.

"Who's the commanding officer here, Private?" Jedidiah asked, swinging stiffly from the saddle and handing his reins to the young man.

"Major Randolph Harris, sir. You'll find him over at the post headquarters," He said, aiming a finger toward a large adobe building on the far end of the parade ground.

"I'll likely be staying until tomorrow. Would you quarter my mounts and allow my dog to sleep in the stall with the pinto? Just hang my saddle and pack on the stall railing. Double grain ration for the horse and mule, nothing for the dog, understand?"

"Yes, sir. He looks more like a wolf instead of a dog, though. Will he..."

"Not unless somebody tries to mess with my stuff or my horses, then he'll take an arm off."

"I'll keep my distance, you can be sure of that."

Jedidiah strode across the parade ground toward the sprawling headquarters building. Two flags flew from the twin poles attached to the bulwark around the roof. One was an American flag. The other was the regimental flag of the Tenth Cavalry.

He pushed through the door. A spit and polish sergeant in full dress sat at a desk just inside the door. He looked up then let his gaze drift down and up and down again. His eyebrows pulled together after a critical appraisal.

"Could I help you?" he asked, his voice suggesting a negative answer to his own question.

"I'd like to see Major Harris."

"I'm afraid Major Harris is a very busy man. What is the nature of your business?"

"Just tell him Jedidiah Boone would like to see him."

"Without an appointment, I'm afraid..."

The sergeant's words were scattered by a man bursting through the front door. He was of medium height, square-faced and clean-shaven. Most of his face was taken up with a wide grin of recognition. The captain's bars on his shoulders brought the desk sergeant out of his seat and snapping to attention.

"Boone?...I thought that was you," the captain said, rushing forward to grab Jedidiah's hand, pumping it repeatedly. "I saw you coming across the parade ground. I couldn't believe my eyes."

"Howdy, Stuart. It's been awhile."

"It sure has. I haven't seen you since the campaign against the Apaches down in Texas. You still scouting for the army? I thought you give it up."

"Did. How'd you manage to get stuck way out here? I figured you for one of those cushy desk jobs in Washington by now."

"Naw. You know me. Like always, I talked when I should have been listening and my superior officer didn't like what he heard, so here I am. What are you doing here?"

"Trying to see the major and not getting very far."

"Wait right here," the Captain, said, turning and walking to a nearby door and tapping on it with a knuckled fist.

"Yes," a voice from beyond the door called out.

Captain Stuart Morgan pushed the door open and stepped inside. A short minute later he stuck his head out again.

"Come on in, Jedidiah."

Major Randolph Harris was not the typical army major. From his years scouting for the army, Jedidiah had come to expect most high-ranking officers to be short, balding, and heavy around the middle. The man that strode confidently around the desk with a hand extended was none of the above.

He looked young for a major, certainly less than forty. Tall and whipcord lean, he walked with his head up and his shoulders square. The brass buttons and belt buckle gleamed against his blue uniform. A small, well-kept mustache decorated his top lip. His deeply tanned face wore a look that was all business.

"Major," Morgan said, "This is an old friend of mine, Jedidiah Boone. Jedidiah, Major Randolph Harris, Commander of the Tenth Cavalry."

The handshake was firm and friendly. Jedidiah's gaze searched the man's eyes and liked what he saw. If he was any judge of a man, this fellow was foursquare.

"Mr. Boone, it's good to meet you. If Captain Morgan calls you a friend, that tells me a lot about you."

"Jedidiah rode with the Second Missouri Cavalry under Colonel Lewis Merill during the war," Captain Morgan explained. "I first met him after the war when he was the chief scout for General George Crook in the Texas campaign against the Apaches."

"The Second Cavalry of Missouri?" Major Harris asked, motioning them to be seated. "Wasn't that the outfit they called the Merill's Horse Raiders?"

"Yes, sir," Jedidiah said, folding into a chair.

"You boys made quite a name for yourselves. Say you scouted for General Crook? I've never met him but I understand he's a man that gets the job done."

"Yes, sir, you could shore say that. He's kind of like a bulldog. He gets a hold of something he don't let go until the fight's over."

"Well, Mr. Boone, what brings you to our little piece of paradise?"

"I'm looking for two white girls that were taken captive about six weeks ago up near Sante Fe. All the signs say it was the Chokonen tribe of the Chiricahua Apache that done it."

"Sante Fe?" the major questioned, his eyebrows wrinkling in surprise. "That's at least three hundred miles to the east?"

"Yes, sir. More like four hundred though. I just rode it."

"You said the signs pointed to the Chokonen tribe of the Chiricahua. That's Cochise's tribe. What signs are you talking about?"

"They hit the ranch just before first light, slit the throats of all the ranch hands while they were still in their bunks. They cut the father's throat, scalped him, and opened up his belly and scattered his guts all over the room, most likely while he was still alive. They raped the woman, scalped her, then cut off both her breasts.

"Far as I know, the Chokonen are the only ones I ever heard of that does that."

"No doubt about it, that's their trademark, all right. Trouble is, they're holed up in a stronghold in the Dragoon Mountains forty miles west of here. We've been fighting them for years. They slip out and make raids, but there's no way they'd go that far. No, there must be some mistake."

"That's what I thought, too," Jedidiah agreed. "But I've got to go where the evidence leads me, and right now it all leads slap-dab to Cochise and his bunch."

"Well," the Major said, shaking his head. "I wish I could help you, Mr. Boone, but I'm afraid I'm going to have to turn down your request. I've only got four hundred men. Most of them are green recruits, not old enough to shave. We estimate Cochise has over a thousand followers in those mountains, two hundred fifty to three hundred of them seasoned fighters.

"The Dragoon Mountains are a literal fortress. My men call it 'hell on earth'. It would take a force of several thousand to go in there and flush him out, even then I'd have my doubts of defeating him without losing half of my men. No, I'm afraid I can't help you."

"Major," Jedidiah said. "With all due respect, I don't recall asking for help. I come here looking for information, not soldiers."

"Then I guess I don't understand, Mr. Boone. What exactly do you plan to do?"

"I plan to go and talk to Cochise and see if his bunch took the girls, if they did, I aim to get them back."

Major Harris exchanged a look of disbelief with Captain Morgan, then focused his gaze again on Jedidiah.

"You can't possibly be serious."

"Oh, yes sir, I'm serious, sure enough. I didn't ride four hundred miles just for the exercise. Major, all I'm asking from you is to tell me all you know about where they're holed up. I'll take it from there."

"I can't let you ride in there, it would be suicide. No. I can't allow it."

"Major Harris, sir, I ain't in your army. I don't see you got a say in where I go," Jedidiah said, irritation clearly showing in his face. He pushed from his chair and stretching to his full height."

"Talk to your friend, Captain. If he rides into the Dragoon Mountains he'll never ride out."

"It'd be a waste of breath," Stuart Morgan said.

"Then sit back down, Mr. Boone. Off the record, I'll help you all we can."

Jedidiah returned to his chair.

"What is it you want to know?" the Major asked, eyeing Jedidiah with a new respect.

"Tell me about his stronghold. Where is it? How do I get there?" Jedidiah asked, fingering his earlobe.

"I don't know. As far as I know, no white man has ever gone into the Dragoons and come back alive. There's only one white man Cochise trusts. His name is Tom J. Jeffords. He's a frontiersman, I guess you'd call him. Don't know if he's ever been to Cochise's stronghold or not. I doubt he'd tell you even if he has."

"Where do I find Jeffords?" Jedidiah asked.

"He's got a cabin southwest of here in the Swisshelm Mountains. His place isn't hard to find. There's a mountain spring, the only water between here and there. His cabin overlooks the spring. If you go, be careful. He's kind of touchy about visitors."

"Thanks, Major," Jedidiah said, rising. "I'm obliged for your help.

"Wish I could do more. I wish you luck, you're sure going to need it."

The first rays of a warm sun creeping through the open window and the street sounds from below woke Julianna from a sound sleep. She jerked to a sitting position in bed, for a moment confused as to where she was. Then she remembered, stretched, and snuggled back down against the pillow. This is wonderful, she thought

A few minutes later she reluctantly rose, walked to the window and swept aside the thin curtain with the back of her hand. The morning sun was just full bright above the horizon. The soft blue sky was spotted with a few white clouds. A gentle breeze puffed through the window and lifted golden curls that cascaded about her shoulder. With a curled finger she flicked a strand from her face.

Sante Fe seemed to just be waking up. A few people were hurrying here and there. A bald headed fellow with an apron tied around his waist was sweeping the boardwalk in front of the mercantile store. A wagon piled high with sacks of feed lumbered by. Two small boys ran after an iron wagon rim and guided it with a forked stick. A dog chased after them playfully.

A tall man in a business suit strode across the street toward the red brick Wells Fargo building. He stepped up onto the boardwalk in front, stopping to talk with another man as he lit a cigar. It was Jedidiah's friend, Winston Taylor. He seemed like such a nice man, she wished she could talk with him about Jedidiah.

I must hurry, she thought. Father had asked them to meet in the lobby at sunrise. They were going to actually eat breakfast in a restaurant. I will be late and father will be upset. She turned from the window and hurriedly poured water from the blue-speckled water pitcher into the matching pan and washed. She put on her clean dress since the only other one she had was dirty from the long trip. Then hurriedly brushed her long hair and rushed downstairs. The family was already waiting.

"I'm sorry I'm late," she tried to explain. "The bed was so comfortable I overslept."

Her mother glanced quickly at her father and smiled.

"It's all right, dear. We were late too."

"Wasn't it neat to have a room all by ourselves," Dewey said excitedly. "When we build our new house, could we all have a room of our own?"

"I'm afraid it won't be that big," their father told them. "But maybe we can manage three bedrooms. We'll see."

They all trooped out of the hotel. Denver and Dewey hurried on ahead. Julianna walked with her mother and father as they crossed the busy street, dodging wagons, buggies, and men on horseback.

"Isn't it exciting," Julianna whispered to her mother as they stepped up onto the boardwalk in front of the Sante Fe Café. "I've never seen so many people at one time in my whole life."

"I don't like the city," Mr. Johnson said. "Too many people."

"But it's a good place to visit now and then," Adrianna suggested. "Wesley, do you suppose Julianna and I could go shopping after breakfast? I'd like to look at some material. I think she needs a new dress now that she has a beau."

"Mother! He's not a beau. He's just...well...I just like him. That's all."

"I suppose we could manage that. If you two will mind your spending. We've got supplies to lay in for the winter."

Julianna was beside herself with excitement as they pushed through the door of the restaurant. A brand new dress! I can't wait until Jedidiah sees me in my brand new dress. So many exciting things are happening so fast.

The restaurant was busy. Most of the tables were crowded, mainly with men. Julianna saw only three other women in the whole room. Her family found a table near the back and the young waiter brought an extra chair. He brought heavy white mugs and poured them full from a blue-speckled coffeepot that matched the water pitcher in her room.

"How may I help you folks this morning?" he asked politely, stealing frequent glances in Julianna's direction.

Wesley Johnson ordered for everyone as if he did it every day of his life. No one would have suspected this was the first and only time his family had ever eaten in a restaurant.

"The boys and I will be busy most of the day loading the supplies Jedidiah ordered," her father said. "I'll swear, it looks to me like he's laying in an awful lot of supplies just for him and his two workers."

"Wesley," Adrianna said, leaning close to her husband. "This is so exciting. Getting to stay in the hotel, actually eat in a restaurant, going shopping, and I can't wait to see the valley Mr. Boone described."

"Now, don't go getting too worked up, Adrianna. We ain't seen that valley yet. It might not be anything like he said it was."

"That friend of his, Mr. Taylor, seems like such a nice man," she said.

"Yeah, he's bending over backwards to see we got everything we need. I even overheard him tell the desk clerk that Wells Fargo would be paying for our stay in the hotel."

"Really? Why would they do that?"

"Don't know, but I'm gonna talk to him about it. I don't want no charity."

"Reckon when we'll be pulling out, pa," Dewey asked.

"If we get the wagons loaded, I'd like to get started at first light. Mr. Taylor is sending two of his men, Mr. Hume and Mr. Honeycutt, to show us the way to Angel Fire Valley. Shore will save us some time hunting it. It'll be good to have them along in case we run into trouble, too."

The waiter brought their food. Their plates were brimming over with ham, scrambled eggs, fried potatoes, biscuits, and fresh honey. They all dug into the food like they were starved.

"Boy! This is shore good," Dewey said around a mouthful of biscuit.

"How does it feel to eat somebody else's cooking, ma?" Denver asked.

"It's very nice," she said, smiling. "Very nice."

Julianna noticed that for the first time since she could remember, her mother had a happy look on her face and a sparkle in her eyes.

After breakfast Mr. Johnson and the boys headed for the General Store to load the supplies. Adrianna and Julianna walked down to the mercantile store to check out the material. They took their time and closely examined most every bolt of material in the store before deciding on light blue gingham. They also purchased several yards of lace to use as trim. They were paying for their purchases when Winston Taylor entered the store.

"Good day, ladies," he said, touching a finger to his hat and smiling. "I trust your rooms at the hotel were satisfactory?"

"Good day, Mr. Taylor," Mrs. Johnson said. "The rooms were very comfortable, thank you."

"I see you ladies are doing some shopping."

"We were just picking out some material for a new dress for Julianna. It's been a long time since we were able to shop."

"I understand you folks are from Missouri?"

"Yes, sir. We were on our way to Colorado with a wagon train but we...we lost our two youngest girls to the fever."

"I see. I'm sorry to hear that. Jedidiah asked me to send someone to guide you to Angle Fire Valley. I'm sending two of my detectives. They've been there before. I understand you'll be leaving in the morning?"

"That's what Wesley said. May I ask how you know Mr. Boone?"

"He and I served together during the war. Then after the war he was a scout for the army. Jedidiah is one of the finest men I've ever met."

"Did Wesley tell you he saved our lives?" Adrianna asked.

"He said Jedidiah rode in while your family was under attack by a band of Comanchero. He didn't tell me any of the details."

"We would have all been killed had he not arrived when he did. He's a very brave man."

"Yes he is. He's saved my life more than once. Both I and Wells Fargo owe him a great debt."

"It seems we are all indebted to him," Adrianna said.

"Miss Johnson," Winston Taylor said, shifting a gaze to Julianna. "Are you going to make your home in the Valley also?"

"Yes, sir. Jedidiah told me how beautiful it is. I'm looking forward to seeing it."

"I've only been there once, but I must say it's one of the most beautiful spots I've ever seen. It's no wonder Jedidiah picked that spot to put down roots. I'm sure you'll be very happy there."

"I believe I will, thank you, Mr. Taylor."

"Well, I'd best be going. If there's anything else I can do for you folks, I'll be over at the Wells Fargo office. Just let me know."

"Thank you, Mr. Taylor," Adrianna said. "You've been very kind."

The wagons were piled high with building supplies, food staples, and feed. The big horses leaned hard into their harness and the wheels cut deep ruts as they pulled out of Sante Fe just after sunup.

The two Wells Fargo detectives rode in front. Adrianna sat proudly beside her husband as he popped the long reins to urge the double team to greater efforts. Julianna rode her blood-red mare alongside the lead wagon. Dewey and Denver drove the second wagon.

"I still can't believe it," Wesley Johnson told his wife, shaking his head in puzzlement. "The store keeper said I didn't owe nothing for all them supplies. Said Wells Fargo had already paid for everything."

"Why would they do that, Wesley?"

"Don't know. I tried to talk to Mr. Taylor about it but he just said it was a down payment on a debt. He wouldn't let me pay a red cent."

"That's strange," Adrianna said. "Have you noticed the glow on your daughter's face since she met that Mr. Boone? It's pretty clear she's got stars in her eyes."

"Far as I can tell he seems like a good sort. He's shore been good to us. From what Mr. Taylor told me though, he's off on a job he ain't likely to come back from."

Chapter Six

"What you looking at through that crack, Elizabeth?" Rebecca asked from behind her.

"I'm just looking to see what I can see."

"I want to see," her little sister said, pushing to get close to the crack in the heavy door.

Elizabeth scooted aside to let Rebecca look. Elizabeth glanced at the scratches on the wall and knew the number without even looking—forty-six. They had been held prisoner forty-six days.

She let out a breath on a ragged sigh. Her heart thudded loud in her chest. The tight, dry knot of hopelessness returned and tugged at her, eating away at her mind. She fought it away as she had so many times before. I must not give up, she thought. I must be strong for Rebecca's sake. The air was so hot it hurt her lungs just to breathe. She wiped a dirty hand across her forehead. She was filthy. In all the time they'd been there, Two Deers Running had taken them down to the stream only once so they could bathe. Elizabeth determined to beg the Indian woman to let them take another bath.

It had been two days since the two Mexican girls had been brought into camp and taken to the little shacks. Elizabeth had seen several of the outlaws going in and out of the two shacks but the girls had never come out. What had those terrible men been doing to them? The unspeakable horrors her mind imagined would be a fate worse than death. Will we be next? Will those horrible men come and drag her and Rebecca to those shacks and do things to them? She determined she'd rather die first.

"They're coming, sis," Rebecca suddenly screamed, terror cracking her small voice. "The ugly men are coming."

Rebecca fled from the door on her hands and knees, cowing on her blanket, trembling, she pulled the covering over her head.

Elizabeth crawled to the door and quickly peeked out the crack. The tall Indian called Nantaje had the older Mexican girl by the arm, dragging her up the hill toward their hut. Her bare feet make bloody trails in the white sand. A big Mexican with a bushy beard stumbled along behind, the younger girl thrown across his shoulder. Both girls were completely naked.

Elizabeth lurched away from the door and threw herself against the wall of the room, her knees hugging her chest. They are coming for us, her mind screamed. What will I do? What can I do?

She waited, straining, quivering. She heard the scuffle of feet outside the door. The bar lifted. The door swung open. Bright light exploded into the room and blinded her for a moment. She turned her face away.

The older girl was flung into the room and went sprawling onto the sandy floor. The big Mexican dumped the younger girl beside Elizabeth. Both girls were covered with blood, their faces battered and swollen.

The big Indian called Nantaje turned. His cold, dark eyes stared at Elizabeth for a long moment, then swung to fix on Rebecca. His hand dropped to the knife at his waist. He slowly drew it out. Sunlight from the door struck the shiny blade and flashed a light beam across the room. He took a slow step toward Rebecca.

Terror clamped its talons deep into Elizabeth's chest. Panic overwhelmed her as the horrible scene of what this monster had done to her mother and father flashed into her mind.

That is the same knife he used to cut open father's stomach! He cut off mother's breasts and scalped her with that knife! Now he was going to scalp Rebecca!

The scream started somewhere deep inside the pit of her stomach. It raced up her throat and burst from her lips in a high-pitched tremor that shattered the thickness of the room. Surging to her feet, she flung herself at the big Indian. The impact jarred her to her bones. Balled fists flailed at him, pummeling him with every ounce of strength in her small body.

A quick backhand swipe landed on the side of her head. A blinding light exploded behind her eyes and sent a starburst of light beams shooting across the sudden blackness of her vision. She felt herself hurtling across the room, landing in a heap on the hard-packed floor. It took all of her remaining strength just to lie there and breathe. She gulped in a great draught of air and tried to blink the world back into focus.

What she saw sent chills spiraling up her spine: One of the Indian's moccasined feet held Rebecca's throat to the floor. One hand grasped her sister's long, golden hair, the other held that gleaming knife. Rebecca's screams pierced the air. Elizabeth couldn't bear to watch. She wanted to turn her face away, to slam her eyes shut, but she couldn't. The knife swept forward, severing a fistful of hair. He had cut off a long lock of Rebecca's hair.

Jedidiah found Tom Jeffords's cabin tucked on a steep slope of the Swiss Helm Mountains just like Major Harris said. It was skirted by a grove of tall trees and overlooked a large pool of crystal clear water. The mountain spring emerged from a small cave, formed an inviting pool then wound its way along the crease in the mountains for a short distance before disappearing back into a crevice as quickly as it appeared.

Reining his horse, he stepped leadenly from the saddle. Keeping an eye fixed on the cabin, he loosened the cinch straps on his animals so they could fill their bellies. Dog lapped thirstily at the water, lifting his big head often to sweep his dark eyes in a wide circle.

As his animals drank, Jedidiah squatted at the water's edge. Reaching a hand, he cupped it full and brought it to his mouth. The water was fresh, sweet, and ice cold.

"Drink your fill, but keep your hands where I can see 'em," a deep voice called.

Jedidiah didn't move anything but his eyes. They darted toward the sound.

The man stood beside a large boulder not thirty yards away. He was tall, rangy, and broad through the shoulders. He wore buckskins similar to Jedidiah's own. His long, flowing brown hair curled around his shoulders and wreathed a sun-darkened face that resembled well-worn saddle leather. A Sharps carbine .45-100 rested comfortably in the crook of an arm.

"I'm looking for Tom Jeffords," Jedidiah said, remaining motionless.

"You found him. Who might you be?"

"Name's Jedidiah Boone."

"What's your business?"

"I stopped at Fort Bowie and talked to Major Harris. He told me you might be able to help me."

"How's that?"

"I'm looking for Cochise. The Major said you were the only white man Cochise trusted. Said you might give me an idea where I could find him."

"Why you looking for him?"

"Some Apaches raided a ranch up near Sante Fe a couple of months ago. Butchered everybody and took two young girls captive.

All the signs say they were from the Chokonen tribe of the Chiricahua Apache. That's Cochise's tribe."

"Signs?...What signs?"

"They cut the man open, scattered his innards all over the place. Cut the woman's breasts off, slashed their throats, then scalped them."

"Sounds like 'em, but it weren't them."

"How do you know that?" Jedidiah asked, still squatting.

"Too far."

"The Major said they often leave their mountain stronghold and go on raids. What makes you think they wouldn't go that far?"

"I know him, that's why. Besides, he wouldn't take no girls."

"You reckon I could stand up without getting shot? I talk better looking a man in the face, besides, I could use a smoke."

"Stand if you want. Man can't be too careful now days. Lives longer that way. Say your name's Boone? No kin to that Daniel Boone fella I heard about, I don't reckon?"

"He was my grandfather's brother," Jedidiah said, stretching to his feet, being careful his hand stayed well away from the .44 Colt on his right leg as he reached for the makings.

"You don't say?"

"So, can you tell me how to find Cochise?"

"Could...won't."

"You got a reason?" Jedidiah asked, taking out the makings and rolling himself a smoke.

"Yep."

"What would that be?"

"It'd get you killed."

"You're a man kinda stingy with words, Mr. Jeffords," Jedidiah said, running his moistened tongue along the edge of a cigarette paper and rolling it in place. He dug a match from his pocket, struck it on his pants leg, and put fire to the twisted cigarette.

"Never liked wasting words," Jeffords said. "Words are like coins. Every one is worth something...man ought not waste them."

"Mr. Jeffords, here's how it is. I aim to find those two little girls. To do that, I need to talk to Cochise. Maybe his bunch didn't do it, maybe they did. Either way, if those girls are still alive, I aim to take them back. I can find him without you but you could save me a lot of time. I'd be obliged for your help."

"You might find him. He'd kill you if you did."

"Maybe so. Everybody's gotta die sometime." Jedidiah said.

Deciding he was wasting his time, he tightened the cinches on his animals and looped Butternut's reins over his neck. Toeing a stirrup, he swung into his saddle.

Jedidiah twisted a quick look when he heard a low growl from deep in Dog's chest. The frontiersman had moved stealthily to within a few feet. His moccasins hadn't made a sound. With a slow hand he removed a beaded ornament from around his neck and held it out to Jedidiah.

"Show them this," Jeffords said. "Tell him I sent you. Maybe he won't kill you."

Leaning down from the saddle Jedidiah took the ornament and turned it in his hand. It was round and flat, about the size of a silver dollar. Yellow interwoven beads depicting the sun were woven into a sky-blue background. Yellow rays ran outward from the sun to the edge. The ornament was suspended on a neck cord of dark blue beads. It was beautiful. He hung it around his neck.

Jedidiah raised his eyes. For a brief moment their gazes locked.

"I'm obliged," Jedidiah said. "How do I find him?"

"Don't fret, friend, he'll find you."

That said, Tom Jeffords turned and walked away. Jedidiah stared after him. The frontiersman walked tall and proud, never once looking back. He's a strange one, that fellow, Jedidiah thought as he reined his pinto around and heeled him into a fast walk, pointing his nose northwest.

* * *

Winston Taylor stood on the boardwalk in front of the Wells Fargo office and watched the Johnson's wagons as they pulled out. Both wagons were heavily loaded with the supplies Jedidiah had asked for in his letter. It was readily apparent most of the supplies on his list weren't for him at all, but for the Johnson family.

It was clear Jedidiah had set his cap for Julianna Johnson. Who could blame him? She was one of the most beautiful women Winston had ever seen. If I were a little younger...Winston thought, as he watched the way she sat the saddle on her red bay mare. Now that's one fine looking woman.

He withdrew a cigar from his inside coat pocket, lit it, and drew in a long inhale, blowing it out in a long, blue trail. He watched idly as the Johnson wagons disappeared in the distance on their way to Jedidiah's Angel Fire Valley. He was glad he had decided to send Hume and Honeycutt to show them the way, he felt easier knowing his two detectives would be watching over them.

Wonder where Jedidiah is? It's been more than six weeks. Does he really stand a chance of getting Mr. Fargo's nieces back? I doubt it. That's more than you could expect from any man.

He decided to walk over to the Sante Fe restaurant and get a cup of coffee. He strode along the boardwalk. A half dozen howdys later he nearly bumped into a man hurrying out of the hotel.

"Homer?" Winston asked. "Homer Douglas? Is that you?"

"Uh...Taylor, isn't it? With Wells Fargo, I believe," the man said, surprise, maybe even shock written all over his face.

"Yes. What are you doing in Sante Fe?" Winston asked. "I haven't seen you since the big meeting in New York a couple of years ago when we closed the deal buying the Butterfield stage line from your boss."

"Yeah, well I...I've got some business here. Mr. Holliday's in the railroad business now, you know."

"I heard something about that. One thing I'll say for your boss, he's a promoter. Sometimes a little unorthodox maybe, but he's always out there hustling some kind of deal."

"Are you still in charge of all the stage operations for Wells Fargo?" Douglas asked. "I thought your office was in San Francisco."

"Oh it is. I was just cleaning up some loose ends here in Sante Fe. Are you going to be around long? Maybe we could get together over dinner?"

"No...I...I'll be leaving on tomorrow's stage. It's good to see you though."

Homer Douglas turned and hurried down the boardwalk. He's an odd sort of fellow, Winston thought. Wonder why he seemed so nervous? Maybe something to do with the business deal he's working on? I wonder what kind of deal it could be? Reckon the railroad's thinking about running a line through Sante Fe? I haven't heard anything about it though.

That's most likely it, they're checking out the possibilities of running their line through here and don't want anyone to know about it. If John Holliday's thinking about bringing his railroad through Sante Fe, Mr. Fargo will want to know about it. I better send him a wire."

Winston puffed on his cigar and watched Homer Douglas hot footing it down the boardwalk. The chubby little man looked kind of funny in his tiny spectacles and that silly looking little bowler hat he wore all the time. He's sure an odd sort of fellow to be John Holliday's right hand man.

Chapter Seven

The Dragoon Mountains rose out of the desert like a festered sore. Jedidiah squinted, shifting his wide brimmed hat lower to shade his eyes against the blinding sun, and surveyed what lay before him. Sunlight bounced off the red sandstone outcroppings that jutted from the earth and blended with the dark outline of trees to create a reddish-purple hue to the distant mountains.

Butternut skirted the thorny creosote bushes and sharp needle spines of the desert yucca plants that dotted the arid land. Small clusters of barrel cactus pointed fingers toward the sky and stood like lonely sentinels guarding the endless expanses of sand.

Jedidiah threw a quick glance over his shoulder at Mule. The Missouri brown plodded faithfully along, the lead rope slack, his head hung low, ears flopping, long tail swishing away the ever present flies. The heavy packsaddle seemed to be in place.

Dog trotted alongside the pinto. His mouth open, tongue lolling, his dark eyes engaged in their constant quest for any impending threat.

Jedidiah slouched against the cantle of his saddle. His hands rested comfortably on the saddle horn. His body rocked to the gentle motion of Butternut's easy gait. He was hot, thirsty, and bone tired.

It shore would be good to be propped back in my rocking chair on the front porch of my cabin right now. I could be sipping a good cup of coffee, watching the mist rise above Angel Fire Falls and listening to the roar of the water as it tumbled over the edge and plunge to the valley floor. Yessir, that shore would be good.

Wonder if Julianna and her family have arrived yet? Maybe they're already there, looking the valley over, deciding where to build their cabin. It shore will seem funny having somebody else in the valley besides Mose and Minnie.

Wesley Johnson seems like a good man, maybe a little green when it comes to surviving on the frontier, but he'll learn.

Those twins are strapping boys. They seem so full of life and energy, kind of like I use to be. Between them and their pa, they ought to be able to put in a good crop come spring.

Julianna's mother is a beautiful woman. I can shore see where Julianna got her good looks. Mrs. Johnson's got a tired, sad look about her. I reckon years of hard work and losing two of her children like she did could do that to a woman. Maybe a new life in the valley will snap her out of it.

Julianne...I never seen a more beautiful woman. I still can't believe she'd give a second look at a saddle tramp like me.

A movement caught his eye and pushed his thoughts aside for another time. A red-tailed hawk drifted in lazy circles against a blue sky. Suddenly it folded its wings and plummeted toward the desert floor, hurtling downward like a rock. It disappeared behind a rolling sand dune up ahead, then climbed back into the sky, dangling a desert rattlesnake in its talons.

That seems the way of it, he thought. The strong prey on the weaker. In a land like this the weak don't last long.

The flat desert gradually gave way to a field of rolling sand hills, climbing higher and higher like a stairway to the mountains up ahead. The landscape was barren, a virtual wasteland. Layers of rock split the sandy earth and angled upward. Stunted mesquite trees somehow survived among great windswept boulders that littered the steep slopes, seemingly forming an impregnable barrier to the mountains that served as Cochise's stronghold.

Jedidiah skirted the edge until he spotted an opening between the rocks and headed for it. His searching gaze scoured the ground for tracks; there were none. That didn't surprise him, any Apache warrior worth his salt knows how to make tracks disappear.

Rock strewn slopes rose sharply on both sides. The faint game trail itself was littered with huge boulders. Butternut had to slowly pick his way through the rocks and around the many spines of the Cholla cactus that would tear at a horse's ankles and render him lame. A man on foot out here was a dead man.

Sparse clusters of bunch grass grew between the rocks and gnarly mesquite. Cactus clung precariously to small splotches of topsoil.

Rivers of molten lava, in eons past, had created fields of black, jagged rock that was literally impassable. A horse's hooves would be cut to ribbons within a few steps.

Jedidiah could quickly see why the soldiers called this place 'Hell on earth'. Cochise had chosen well. It was a place ready-made for ambush. Ten Apache could be within a few feet of you and you'd never know they were there. One man with a good rifle could hold off two dozen attackers. It was said Cochise had at least two hundred fifty battle-tough warriors. No wonder the army wasn't anxious to tangle with them.

"Go on ahead, Dog," he instructed his trail companion, lifting an arm to arch forward.

Jedidiah flicked a glance upward at the searing sun, which beat down with a brassy glare. It hung mid-way of its downward arch.

Since mid morning he had been picking his way through the mountains without any sign of life whatsoever.

Rounding a bend in a crease between the mountains, Jedidiah came face-to-face with a deep canyon. Sheer walls fell hundreds of feet and were a rainbow of layered colors: reds, black, and a rusty brown. At the bottom of the canyon, angrily fighting its way to the sea, lay the muddy Salado River.

Casting about, his only available route was along the lip of the canyon to his left. He reined that way. Overhead, dark specs scribed circles in the sky, drifting lazily on an updraft from the canyon in their never ending search for food. He hoped the appearance of the desert scavengers wasn't a bad omen.

He swallowed dry. Their last water had been the spring back at Thomas Jeffords place. That had been yesterday afternoon. His animals had to have water soon.

Reining up in a small clearing among a jumble of rocks and mesquite bushes, he climbed wearily from the saddle. He retrieved one of his four canteens from Mule's packsaddle. Uncorking it, he tipped it to his cracked lips. It was hot, but washed the dust down his scratchy throat and felt good.

Swiping off his hat, he poured the bottom full of the life saving liquid and held it for Butternut. The pinto quickly swigged the hat dry. Repeating the process, he allowed Mule a few sips before pouring some for Dog.

"I know that ain't enough, big fellow," Jedidiah said soothingly, as the wolf dog looked up at him, pleading eyes begging for more. "No telling when we'll be able to get to all that water down there in the canyon."

Dog's head suddenly shot around, the hair on his neck stood on end and a low warning growl rumbled deep inside his chest; they had company.

Jedidiah stiffened. Shooting a glance, he stared right into the dark eyes of a dozen Apache warriors. They had materialized magically from behind scattered rocks.

Their bronzed skin glistened in the sun. They were naked except for a breechcloth and knee-high moccasins. Their long black hair was held in place by twisted red pieces of cloth, the mark of an Apache warrior. Each held a rifle aimed squarely at him.

Swallowing a lump from his throat into a churning stomach, he fought back the instinct to go for his gun. His mind whirled. He knew he had only an instant to decide. If he fought, what would be accomplished? He would certainly take some of them with him but in the end he would die. How would that help the girls? No, this was the time for words, not guns. If he was to survive, words must be his weapon. Slowly he raised his empty hands.

Beside him, Dog rumbled that low, menacing growl deep inside his chest. Jedidiah knew the sound. He knew Dog was about to attack. But he also knew it would be useless. The Indians would kill him and eat him. Dog meat was one of their favorite foods. The only way to save his companion was to send him away.

"Dog!" he whispered loudly without turning his head. "Go!"

The big wolf dog paused for only an instant, then wheeled and headed back the way they had come in a dead run. Rifles barked. Bullets kicked up dust all around him. A rifle slug ricocheted off a boulder as Dog disappeared behind it. He had escaped.

Stepping from behind the rocks the Indians quickly surrounded Jedidiah. A barrel-built warrior relieved him of his pistol and Bowie knife. Another gathered Butternut's reins.

"I came to..."

A rifle butt to the back of his head halted his words. Flashing explosions of light interrupted his vision. He blinked furiously to drive away the lights. He felt himself falling. A dark shroud of blackness settled over him.

Awareness fought to return but only partially succeeded. He

recognized the sensation of movement. Floating...he was floating. He strained to force open his eyes...his head was bursting...he saw only a blur...the world was upside down. Swaying...his body seemed to be swaying. A sharp, throbbing pain pounded inside his head. Sound reached him...the click of horses' hooves on rock. His arms were hanging below his head...his hands were bound together...he was hanging across his own saddle. How long he rode like that he didn't know...he drifted in and out of consciousness...his head pounded...his vision blurred.

Once he was shocked half awake by water-lots of water. It was as if the sky suddenly opened up and dumped hundreds of buckets on him all at once-then it stopped-still they rode on.

It was dark when someone dumped him from the saddle. He landed on a cushion of soft grass. The world spun crazily. His mind whirled. He couldn't think straight. His wrists were jerked far out to his side. Strands of leather quickly secured them to some kind of stake in the ground. His legs were stretched out and secured.

He struggled with all his might to force his eyelids open. Everything was out of focus. Flames leaped into the air from a nearby fire. Blurred figures milled about. Then he realized-he was spread-eagled and staked out in an Apache camp.

He had to tell them. He opened his mouth to speak-no words came out. What is wrong with me? He tried again. He must scream out to them. He must tell them he wanted to talk to Cochise. His mind willed his mouth to speak. His lips moved but no sound reached his ears.

Staked out—he had seen it before. He'd come across bodies of men the Apaches had staked out, or at least what was left of them. It was a favorite game. They spread-eagled a man, taunted him, tormented him and enjoyed their favorite sport of torture to see how much their victim could stand.

It was a ritual, a celebration of victory over an enemy. They often drank mescal, danced, and when they had worked themselves into frenzy, the climax came. They slit their victim's stomach, pulled out handfuls of intestines, and stretched them out as far as they would reach...then they calmly sat down to watch the victim slowly die...the longer it took...the greater the value of the scalp.

When would it happen? Tonight...tomorrow...no telling...but it would happen.

The night wore on. His head was splitting, pounding like a drum. I must have a concussion, reason told him. Sharp pains shot from the back of his head and raced through his whole body. He slipped in and out of consciousness. He couldn't concentrate.

He felt himself drifting...floating...his mind looked down and saw his body...and he didn't hurt anymore. The sweet peace of blackness closed around him...

Something touched his cheek...soft, wet. His mind pried his eyes open. It was Dog. The big wolf dog stood beside him. His tongue flicked out, licking his master's face.

Jedidiah lay flat of his back, his hands and feet tied securely to the stakes. It was still dark. His head hurt, but not as bad as before. He rolled his head. His gaze swept a circle around the Apache camp. All was quiet.

"Good boy," he said without thinking, then hearing the sound of his own voice, felt an overwhelming elation. I can talk again! My voice has returned. Now I can tell them...but will they listen? Will they understand? Will they let me talk to Cochise?

Time crept slowly. There was nothing to do but wait until morning. He tried to relax...to rest. Dog lay down beside him and rested his head on Jedidiah's stomach.

"I've shore got myself in a pickle this time, big fellow," Jedidiah told his companion. "It wasn't your fault. You warned me. Maybe come morning I can get them to let me talk to Cochise. I got a feeling that's my only hope."

The wolf dog raised his big head at the sound of his master's voice. Jedidiah could feel those dark eyes staring at him as if trying to understand. Jedidiah drew comfort from Dog's presence, but he knew he had to send him away. If the Apaches caught him, without a doubt, they would kill him.

"I hate to do it," Jedidiah told his faithful companion, "but I've got to...Go!" he whispered in a firm voice.

The big dog climbed to his feet, turned, and trotted a few feet away and stopped. His big head swiveled back. His dark eyes stared. Jedidiah thought they looked sad.

"Go!" Jedidiah said firmly, his voice breaking.

For a long moment the dog hesitated, then wheeled and disappeared into the darkness.

Unbelievably, Jedidiah slept. How long he slept he had no idea. When he awoke it was still dark, black dark, the dark that comes just before dawn. The night gave up grudgingly as if it was trying to forestall the events the day would bring. He watched the first blush of dawn creep over the crest of a nearby mountain. As the gray sky gradually brightened, the lodges of a large Apache village came into view.

All was quiet. A light breeze touched his face—soft like a lover's gentle caress. The happy sound of a bird chirped from a nearby tree. Somewhere in the village a dog barked. It was a warm, fall dawn with a pearly sky and a scent of pine in the air. It promised to be a better day than most for a man to die.

He closed his eyes and listened to the silence around him. In the darkness behind his closed eyes he thought of Julianna. So beautiful...so perfect. A man could live ten lifetimes and never meet a woman like that. Now, just as he found her, he was about to lose her without the chance to share their lives. Without the chance to dream dreams, to plan, and to work to make those dreams come true. It wasn't fair to lose something so precious just as you found it.

A sense of fatalism stole over him. He would die today. Having no future meant he had few choices. One choice remained to him: he could choose how he would die. If he had to die, he determined he would do it with dignity. Having arrived at that decision, a peace occupied him.

Elizabeth held her little sister for a long time after the ugly Indian left. Tears coursed trails down Rebecca's dirty face and wet the front of Elizabeth's doeskin dress. Great sobs wracked her frail body. Elizabeth's own eyes burned with salty tears. They clung to each other, each of them sapping what little strength remained in the other.

Questions Elizabeth had smothered with her grief and drowned in her tears slithered to the front of her mind. Why had the one called Nantaje cut off a lock of Rebecca's beautiful hair? Why were they holding them prisoner?

Outside, she heard footsteps. The bar lifted from the door. Was he coming back? Elizabeth cringed inside. The door opened and Two Deers Running stepped through. She was carrying a bucket of water and a handful of rags.

She cast a long look at Elizabeth and Rebecca, then turned her attention to the two Mexican girls that lay motionless nearby. The younger of the two seemed either unconscious or...maybe dead. The older one rolled her head back and forth and cried.

Two Deers Running knelt beside the smaller girl and placed an ear against her chest, listening intently. She dipped a rag into the bucket and began bathing blood from the girl's battered face. Moving the wet cloth gently, soothingly, she mopped the blood and dirt from the girl's face. Again and again she dipped the bloody rag in the bucket and wrung it out, coloring the water a crimson red.

When she finished with the younger girl, she turned her attention to the older of the two. She bathed her from head to toe in the bloody water, then, leaning close, she gathered the sobbing girl in her arms and spoke quietly and soothingly, like a mother would comfort her own child.

Elizabeth's heart went out to the Mexican girls. A sob of sympathy worked its way up her throat and lodged there. How could anyone be so cruel? How could those men have done what she could only imagine they did?

Two Deers Running stayed for a long time. Finally, she pushed to her feet and, without a word, hurried out the door.

"Are you all right?" Elizabeth whispered after a few moments, not knowing if the older girl even understood English.

The girl's dark eyes flicked toward her, rounded with surprise and fright. Elizabeth realized the girl hadn't even known anyone else was in the room. The eyes softened but she didn't reply. She just dropped her chin to her chest and slowly shook her head, at least she had understood.

Rebecca lay curled into her familiar fetal position and lapsed into a withdrawn state, now and then sobbing quietly. Elizabeth felt an overwhelming need to somehow reach out to her fellow prisoner, to console the wounded and battered girl. On hands and knees, Elizabeth made her way over to sit beside her.

As her mother had done so many times for her, Elizabeth encircled the girl's shoulder with an arm and pulled her head to her. She couldn't think of any comforting words so she just held her close.

"Is she your sister?" Elizabeth asked softly.

The girl lifted her head from Elizabeth's shoulder and looked at the younger girl for a long moment before answering.

"Si, she is my sister. Her name is Rosa. Do you think she will ever wake up?

"Two Deers Running seemed to think so."

"My name is Christine Ramirez. Who are you?"

"I'm Elizabeth Fargo. That's my little sister over there. Her name is Rebecca. We were taken captive forty-seven days ago from our ranch near Sante Fe. Did they kill your parents too?"

"Si, and my brother also. They are mucho malo men. They do malo things to us."

"I'm so sorry," Elizabeth told her sincerely. "Why don't you lie down over there on my blanket and try to get some rest. Maybe Two Deers Running will bring more blankets and something to eat before long."

After the girl finally drifted off to sleep, Elizabeth sat for a long time, staring at the three sleeping girls, wondering what was going to happen to them.

It was good daylight before the Apache camp began to wake. Jedidiah rolled his head and watched the women as they coaxed cooking fires to life in front of their small, round-top wickiups. Within minutes the whole village was alive with activity.

Indian women dressed in doeskin dresses, their long black hair hanging to their waists, busied themselves preparing food over the fires. Some passed within a few feet of him. He called out, trying to get their attention, but they only turned their heads, refusing to look at him for some unknown reason.

One old man shuffled up to where Jedidiah was staked out. His gray streaked hair was plaited and hung down his back. His face was wrinkled and his lips sunken where teeth used to be. He stared at Jedidiah through tired, curious eyes.

"Cochise," Jedidiah tried. "I've got to talk to Cochise. Can you help me?"

Whether the old man understood, or even heard, Jedidiah couldn't tell. No reaction showed on his leathered face. After a moment the man simply turned and walked away.

Jedidiah's arms and legs were numb; all feeling had long since left them. He was so thirsty he couldn't even make spit. His lips were cracked and bleeding. His tongue felt swollen as big as his hand. His throat was scratchy. It hurt just to move his head and he could tell there was a big knot on the back.

From what he could see, the village was located in an enclosed valley. He couldn't see full circle around him, but from what he could tell, it looked to be maybe a half mile or so across. Sheer walls climbed three hundred feet into the air on all sides. He saw tall pine, paloverde, and cottonwood trees. The ground was covered with thick, green grass. Wherever this place is, it sure ain't like the country I've been seeing the last couple of days. One thing for sure, I'm inside Cochise's hideout. Getting out? Now that don't look too promising.

The fiery red sun finally discovered the hidden valley and peeked its head over the mountain rim. Jedidiah wished it hadn't. The first rays touched his face and he felt its heat immediately on his skin. Within minutes, sweat poured from his face, draining what little moisture remained in his body. Sweat trailed into his hair and soaked it wringing wet. He shuttered his eyes and rolled his head away to filter out the blinding light.

Time inched by...

The soft crunch of moccasin clad footsteps reached his hearing. He blinked the fuzzy forms into focus and saw three Apache warriors. They stood around him, staring down at him through dark eyes.

The biggest of the three was as tall as Jedidiah himself. He had wide shoulders, a huge chest, and heavily muscled arms. His long, coal-black hair was held in place by a bright red bandanna across his forehead and framed a chiseled face and square jaw. A slash of mouth had a cruel turn to his lips. His cold looking, penetrating eyes bored holes in Jedidiah.

"I Ochobee," the Indian said in broken English, pounding a fisted hand on his massive chest. "I scalp leader of Chiricahua. Many white men's scalps hang on my scalp pole. When sun rests, your scalp will hang highest in front of my wickiup."

That said, all three Apaches spun and started away.

"Wait!" Jedidiah screamed. "I came to talk to Cochise. I must talk to him!"

They stopped. The one that had spoken turned and glared at Jedidiah a long moment before answering.

"Cochise not here. Why you want talk?"

"Here...under my shirt. There's something I need to show you. It's some sort of medal. I'm supposed to show it to Cochise."

"Cochise not here," the man said strongly, then wheeled and walked away.

The message of the man's words rang through his mind. Jedidiah knew all to well what it meant. In the Unites States army, the stripes on a man's sleeve or the bars on his shoulders determine a soldier's rank.

In the Chiricahua Apache belief, two things determine a warrior's rank: the number of scalps that hang on his scalp pole that stands in front of his wickiup, and more importantly, the position of each scalp on the pole. The greater the victim suffered before dying, the higher position his scalp occupies on the pole.

Ochobee had promised Jedidiah's scalp would occupy the highest position...when the sun rests...

The sun cooked into him. His face was afire. Even through his closed eyelids the searing light blinded him. He could feel his strength ebbing away.

By the time the blazing inferno stood straight overhead Jedidiah was having trouble staying awake. His confused mind told him he should just allow himself to sleep and never wake up, a much easier way to die than what he faced.

Somewhere nearby the sound of a beating drum began, then another. He struggled to pry his eyes open. He saw nothing but a blinding light. He tried to scream over the sound of the drums, but only a dry, raspy sound came from his throat. His parched and cracked lips mouthed words, but even he couldn't recognize the mumbled sounds.

He lapsed into unconsciousness...

Through the dark cobwebs of his mind he clawed his way back. Sounds drifted to him from far away, as if from a deep cavern, echoing, bouncing off the walls of his half conscious state.

Reaching...searching...grasping, he fought to find something...anything to grab hold of...something solid to pull him back to full awareness. All around him he gradually became aware of activity. Pounding drums, dancing men. Somewhere a voice chanted a monotone refrain.

Realization came, and he wished it hadn't. It was beginning...the celebration of death had begun...and he was the guest of honor.

Chapter Eight

Wesley Johnson and his son, Dewey, were busy watering and picketing the horses. Denver was off in the edge of the woods chopping wood for the night and morning fire. Julianna and her mother were busy preparing supper.

On a log beside the campfire, the two Wells Fargo detectives sat sipping coffee. As usual, they didn't turn a hand to help with the chores. Julianna was fully aware of Detective Hume's hungry eyes. They had followed every move she made ever since they left Sante Fe. She had tried to ignore it at first, thinking it would stop, but it had only grown steadily worse.

Twice he had ridden up beside her and tried to engage her in conversation. She had tried to be civil, but his suggestive comments had been more than obvious. Since then, she had gone to great lengths not to be alone with him.

"Mother," she whispered as they stood behind the wagon from the two detectives. "I...That man, Detective Hume, he's making me very uncomfortable the way he keeps staring at me."

"I know, honey. I've noticed it. I just don't know what to do about it. I'm afraid of what might happen if I told your father. They said we'd be there by noon tomorrow. Let's just see if we can ignore him until then."

Julianna's father and the twins finished their chores and washed up for supper. Mr. Johnson poured himself a cup of coffee and squatted near the fire.

"What kind of work does detectives do for Wells Fargo," he asked.

"It depends," James Hume said, his gaze fixed intently upon Julianna as she set the tin plates and spoons on the drop-leaf attached to the back of one of the wagons. "If there's a stage holdup, we have to go catch the outlaws. If somebody is stealing from one of our offices, we find out who it is and turn them over to the law."

"That must be exciting work," Dewey chimed in.

"Yeah, I guess so." Hume replied.

"You ever shoot anybody?" the boy asked.

"Son," his father said. "That ain't a proper question to ask somebody."

"Let the boy be," Hume said sharply. "Ain't nothing wrong in asking if a man knows how to use a gun. Yeah, boy. I've killed men, four at last count."

"Mr. Jedidiah killed nine Comanchero and saved our lives," Dewey bragged proudly. "If he hadn't come along we'd a been goners for sure."

"Yeah," Hume said sarcastically, shooting a mocking look aimed at Julianna. "I reckon some think he's the cock of-the walk around these parts. One of these days somebody's gonna see just how tough he really is."

"He shore has been good to us," Wesley Johnson said, kind of meekly.

"Seems so," Hume said. "Ain't that right, Missy?"

Julianna was busy taking hot biscuits out of the Dutch oven. She heard the comment and knew he was talking to her, but she pretended not to hear him.

"I said!" Hume raised his voice, anger building in it. "I

reckon Jedidiah Boone must have been mighty good to you, wasn't he, Missy?"

Julianna decided she could ignore him no longer. Though usually soft-spoken, she had a streak in her backbone that few had witnessed. Proudly, she stiffened her spine and determinedly wheeled to face him. Anger boiled up from somewhere deep inside her and blossomed crimson red on her face. Her heart beat like the wings of a hummingbird. Her green eyes flashed. Her jaw set. When she spoke the words came out like poison darts.

"Yes, Mr. Hume. Jedidiah was very good to me. In fact of matter, when he returns, I intend to marry him. I doubt neither he nor Mr. Taylor would take kindly to either your words or your suggestive looks."

Julianna's sudden outburst rendered the detective speechless in fact, it rendered the whole Johnson family speechless...it was a very quiet supper.

All morning the excitement had been building. Julianna had ridden beside her father and mother's wagon since setting out just before sunrise. She hadn't wanted to allow an opportunity for detective Hume to get her alone.

They traversed great stands of forested areas where colorful fall trees rustled in the wind. They crossed crystal mountain streams so cold one couldn't hold his hands in them. They stopped in meadows high with grass that lay lush and green in the sun. With each turn of the wagon wheel, anticipation grew and the pounding in Julianna's chest got louder.

They heard the falls before they saw them. It began as a low, distant rumbling, and gradually became a constant roar.

The pine trees were the tallest and biggest Julianna had ever seen. She leaned far back in the saddle, her gaze following the massive trunks into the sky. The majesty of the giants closed around them. Silence descended, the cushioned softness of the thick grass muffled every sound except the growing rumble of the falls up ahead.

Then they saw it...

Breaking out from the cover of the big trees and into the open meadow they saw Angel Fire Falls. She reined her mare to a stop. Julianna's heart leaped. Her mouth dropped open. She caught her breath in a ragged gasp.

Her father hauled the horses to a stop. The sun rose near noon. For long minutes they sat motionless, staring at the indescribable sight. A river of water tumbled over the edge of the mountain and plunged several hundred feet. The roiling whitewater hurtled downward, landing with a deafening roar. A perfect rainbow arched over the top of the falls, crowning it with multiple layers of color. The sight was breathtaking.

"I've never seen anything so beautiful," Julianna's mother finally breathed out.

Not knowing what the holdup was, the twins jumped down from their trailing wagon and ran up beside the lead wagon. Suddenly they stooped dead in their tracks and joined the rest of the family as they stared...speechless at the sight.

"Gol-lee," Dewey said, his eyes rounded in awe. "Is this where we're gonna live?"

"This is where we're gonna live," their father said proudly without diverting his gaze from the sight.

James Hume had pulled in his horns since Julianna's dressing down the night before. He and his partner had ridden stirrup-to-stirrup all morning, often talking in low tones and completely ignoring the family, which suited the Johnsons just fine. No one noticed when the two reined around and walked their horses back toward the wagons.

"We did our job," Detective Hume said, with a somewhat meeker tone than he had used the night before. "We're heading back."

"Tell Mr. Taylor we're obliged for your help," Mr. Johnson said.

As the two Wells Fargo men disappeared from sight back up the trail, Wesley Johnson fixed his daughter with a gaze.

"Now, young lady. I'd like to know exactly what you meant when you said you are going to marry Jedidiah Boone?"

"I meant what I said, father. Jedidiah just don't know it yet."

Winston Taylor sat in the big office on the second floor of the Wells Fargo building. He had a stack of paperwork several inches high and growing every day. He knew there was no way he could oversee the entire Wells Fargo stage line operation from Sante Fe. He also knew Mr. Fargo expected him to stay right where he was until the kidnapping matter was resolved.

He removed a cigar from the humidor on his desk, bit off the end, and put fire to one of the few luxuries he allowed himself. Leaning back and drawing a long inhale, he let the smoke linger, and enjoyed the rich, sweet rush of pleasure he always experienced from a fine cigar.

Lately, he'd been spending most of his days sending and receiving telegrams. Mostly explaining to Mr. Fargo that he still hadn't heard anything. It's been near two months now, and I still haven't heard a word from Jedidiah. I'm running out of excuses to give Mr. Fargo.

A light tap on the door scattered his thoughts.

"Yes," he called out.

It was one of the young clerks from the office downstairs. The young man timidly stepped through the door and stood just inside, fidgeting.

"Yes, Norman. What is it?"

"Mr. Taylor, sir. There's an old Indian downstairs. He says...I mean...I wasn't sure...

"What is it, Norman? Just say whatever it is."

"Well, sir. This old Indian says he's got a message for you."

"An Indian...with a message for me? Well, don't just stand there Norman, show him up."

"Yes sir," the young man said and hurried from the office.

Why on earth would an Indian be bringing me a message? Winston rose and stepped to the window. Peering down, he saw a broken down old horse tied to the hitching rail in front of the office. It stood with its head near touching the ground and was slat-ribbed. Even from the upstairs window he could count the ribs along the horse's side. There was no saddle, only a single rein hackamore, and a worn out Indian blanket thrown across the horse's back

He turned when the door pushed open and Norman showed the old Indian inside. Winston wasn't good at judging ages, but he would have been afraid to even guess this man's. He was bow-legged, stoop backed, and his face was covered with deep wrinkles. The solid gray hair was plaited and hung down his back. In his hand he carried a small leather pouch.

"I am called, Running Bear," the old man said in broken English. "One of daughters is squaw of Amos Hobbs. You know?"

"No," Winston told him. "I'm afraid not."

"Amos Hobbs has trading post on Rio Grande River. His friend, Jedidiah Boone, say two white girls stole by Apache. Three suns ago, Apache bring pouch. Amos Hobbs tell me bring to Taylor at Wells Fargo office. I bring."

"Wait," Winston told him, hurrying to the door and hollering for the clerk. Young Norman took the stairs two at a time.

"Norman, I want you to take this man over to the general store and buy him whatever he wants. Food, a new blanket, clothes, anything he wants...except whiskey of course."

After they left, Winston Taylor sat down and opened the pouch. Inside he found a wadded up young girl's nightgown with small blue flowers on it. He could only assume it was the one Elizabeth Fargo had been wearing the night she was kidnapped.

He also found a folded paper. Fingering it open, he gazed down at a large lock of golden hair. That has to be Rebecca's hair, he decided. He read the note out loud.

We have the girls. If you want them back alive wells fargo must do the following:

1. Withdraw from bidding on nationwide government mail contract.

2. Bring $50,000 in gold double-eagles to the old abandoned Gran Quivira mission by sundown on October 15. If more than one man shows up or if nobody shows up the girls will be killed...

For a long space of time he sat there, staring at the nightgown and lock of hair. He read the note several times.

First off, just as Jedidiah had suspected, it was now abundantly clear it wasn't the Apaches that kidnapped the Fargo girls; the Apache don't send ransom notes. Second, October 15 was less than three weeks away.

Grabbing a pen and paper, he scribbled a quick telegram to Mr. Fargo in San Francisco telling him everything and asking for instructions about what he should do. There was no time to lose.

In less than two hours the reply came. Winston anxiously took the telegram from the delivery boy and read it.

I agree to all terms. Will arrive on October 10 with the money. Make necessary arrangements to deliver as demanded.

William G. Fargo

Winston's mind whirled.

Mr. Fargo is going to meet the kidnappers' demand. He's going to withdraw from the mail contract negotiations and pay the money. But even if he does, will the kidnappers release the girls? I doubt it. But I would do the same thing if they were my nieces.

Who could be behind this? It's got to be somebody

wanting that contract awfully bad to do something like this...but who? Since Wells Fargo bought the Butterfield stage line two years ago, there's not another line big enough to handle a nationwide contract like that.

Jedidiah was right all along. He said this thing didn't smell right from the start. Wonder where he is? Wonder if he'll be back in time to deliver the ransom money? If not, who will take it to the kidnapers? Me? Or maybe Detective Hume? I'll let Mr. Fargo decide that when he gets here.

Jedidiah lapsed into semi-consciousness. A cruel twist of fate had awakened him for his final date with death. It was past dusky dark but he lay in a circle of light. All around him campfires blazed, licking fingers of flame toward a darkened sky. The drums beat with a growing intensity...building...steadily building...as if toward a final crescendo.

Just outside the jagged circle of light semi-nude men gyrated in a ritualistic dance of death. In their hands they clutched long knives. The shiny blades captured the firelight and flashed it off into the night.

As the dancers circled the fire, they let out blood curdling screams and leaped across the flames into the enclosure where Jedidiah lay. Their hands flashed out, slashing the razor-sharp blades at him, intentionally missing by a fraction of an inch, then leaping back across the wall of flames.

Jedidiah had heard the narrative of the ritual many times. He knew the end was near. When the drums stopped the warrior in the circle would be Ochobee...and his knife wouldn't miss.

Jedidiah tensed. He willed his eyes open, forcing the sunburned lids apart; he wanted to see the end when it came. I will not scream...! I will not scream...! I will not allow myself to make a sound. He made a final promise to himself. His ears felt the building rhythm. His body quivered in anticipation...

A tall, muscled body hurtled the flames.

It was as if time slowed down. Jedidiah saw the dark form as it sailed over the wall of fire. He watched, as the figure seemed to hover as if suspended in the air above him. Ever so slowly it descended. The ground seemed to shudder when the Indian landed.

The drums stopped. Suddenly there was total silence. Recognition fought its way to the surface of Jedidiah's clouded mind...It was Ochobee!

He stood astride Jedidiah, one foot planted on either side. His greased body glistened in the flickering firelight. His muscles rippled. He raised both hands high in the air. Firelight danced on the long, shiny blade of the knife clutched in his hand.

A deathly silence held the whole valley captive. Not a sound marred the moment. Then the stillness was shattered by a scream like no other Jedidiah had ever heard. He braced for what he knew would come next. His eyes followed the path of the big knife as it flashed downward. He clenched his teeth, determined no sound would breach their barrier. His body stiffened, his stomach muscles knotted.

He was about to die.

The knife's tip threaded underneath Jedidiah's buckskin shirt and razored upward, parting the soft animal skin and leaving a thin trail of blood in its wake. The shirt fell apart. The hand clutching the knife shot into the air again. It seemed to poise, as if building energy for a second journey downward; this time it would part Jedidiah's stomach as easily as it severed the thin piece of material.

Firelight lit the area inside the circle brighter than a thousand candles, illuminating the blue and yellow medal that hang around Jedidiah's neck, the medal Thomas Jeffords had given him.

"Wait!" a deep voice of authority from outside the circle of flame ordered.

The knife hand stopped in mid-air.

A portion of the wall of flames was raked aside. Another dark figure stepped through the opening. He paused beside Jedidiah. Leaning down, he lifted the medal, turning it slowly with his fingers.

Jedidiah's heart refused to disturb the silence by beating...a long moment passed.

"Release him!" the voice ordered.

Ochobee wheeled and stalked angrily from the circle.

Jedidiah closed his eyes. He let out his captured breath in a long, slow, slide of air. A sense of relief washed through him, so wondrous and sweet, so tangible and strong, it stole his breath away. He swooned into half consciousness.

He felt his hands and feet being set free. He was barely aware of being lifted...carried...and placed on a soft bed of fur. Feminine hands bathed him; gentle hands applied a salve, soothing his sunburned face and lips. Patient hands gave him water and food.

Time ministered to him. Dark became light again and again. People came. People went away. He slept.

It had been three days since Christine and Rosa were brought to the little shack. Two Deers Running had provided extra food and water as well as blankets for the two Mexican girls. Elizabeth had bathed their wounds regularly and they seemed to be starting to heal. More importantly, their spirits seemed to be improving.

The presence of the Mexican girls boosted Rebecca too. She no longer sat and stared; she joined into the conversation. A bond seemed to be forming among the four girls.

They decided to take turns keeping watch through the crack in the door. All day they watched, relaying every movement in the camp to the other three.

It was early morning, not long after good light. Rebecca happened to be on watch.

"They're all getting on their horses," she said. "Looks like all of them are leaving."

"Count them," Elizabeth told her sister. "See how many there are."

For a long minute Rebecca didn't speak.

"Fourteen," she finally said. "Scarface was with them, too."

"Wonder where they go?" Christine said. "I hope they don't go to hurt someone. I hope they don't bring back other girls and do those things to them."

"Here comes Two Deers Running," Rebecca said excitedly.

"Wonder what she's coming for"? Elizabeth asked. "It's too early for her to bring our food."

Rebecca scooted away from the crack in the door as the bar was lifted. The door swung open. The Indian woman seemed excited. She motioned hurriedly with her hand, urging them to follow her.

"They all gone," she said. "You bathe in river."

Elizabeth couldn't believe her ears. Only once in the fifty-three days had they been allowed to bathe. Excitement found birth in her stomach and surged through her body. It was like they had suddenly been given a great gift.

It was like recess at school. The four girls burst from the cabin. They ran and stumbled down the incline toward the river, laughing, screaming in happiness.

Reaching the water's edge, they plunged into the waist-deep pool, splashing happily in the cool water. Elizabeth ducked under, allowing the delicious liquid to completely surround her with its soft, silky presence; it was wonderful.

The four girls washed themselves even as they laughed and played. Forgetting for a few moments where they were...shutting out of their minds not only the things that had happened to them, but also the horrible things that the future might hold for them.

Two Deers Running sat on the bank and watched the four girls as they bathed and romped in the water. All too quickly time passed and she herded them from the river and back toward their tiny prison. Still, they returned with a clean body, a fresh energy, and a closer bond with each other.

The excitement of the previous day was quickly forgotten early the next morning. Elizabeth was on watch. She saw two Mexican Comanchero head up the hill toward their cabin. Two others watered five horses down beside the river. Somehow, she knew immediately it meant something bad. The words caught and nestled in Elizabeth's chest, refusing to be spoken, as if delaying their saying would somehow forestall what she feared was about to happen. She had to swallow a big lump in her throat before she could speak.

"Two of them are coming," she announced sadly, believing the worst.

Jedidiah awoke in stages. His hearing brought the sounds of an awakening camp to his consciousness: a barking dog, a crying baby, and a happy child's laughter. A gentle breeze wafting through the door opening brought the scent of morning's freshness and cooking food. His sixth sense told him of another presence even before he blinked his eyes into focus.

In the doorway of the wickiup stood an imposing figure. He was lithely muscled, well built, above average height for an Apache, with lean flanks and broad shoulders. He wore buckskin pants and a beaded buckskin shirt. A breechcloth hung over his pants almost to his knees. Several strands of colorful beads draped around his neck. His long, black hair was held in place with a bright red headband. He stared at Jedidiah with a long, steady gaze.

"I am Cochise," he said in near-perfect English. "How are you called?"

Jedidiah licked his lips before answering and was surprised to find them almost healed.

"Jedidiah Boone."

Cochise raised a hand and opened it. The colorful medal

Thomas Jeffords had given him rested in the brown palm.

"Where did you get this?"

"Thomas Jeffords gave it to me. He said to show it to you. Seems I almost didn't get the chance. What is it?"

"It is the Metal of Life. It is the highest sign of honor an Apache can bestow on another. It assures the wearer no harm will come to him by the hands of The People. Thomas Jeffords is the only white man ever to receive one. By giving it to you, he has given you the gift of life and forfeited that right for himself."

Jedidiah pushed to a sitting position and thought on what had just been said. Until that moment, he hadn't realized the enormity of what Jeffords had done for him. He owed the frontiersman his life.

Cochise stepped forward and folded easily into a cross-legged sitting position.

"Why have you come?" he asked.

Jedidiah took his time with the answer. He explained about the raid, about the methods used in the killings, about the kidnapping of the two girls.

"I didn't believe your people would raid that far," he explained, "but all the evidence seemed to point that way. I had to come and find out. I have heard you are a man of truth. I'm asking you. Do you have the girls?"

"Jedidiah Boone is a very brave man. I have great respect for bravery...and for truth. No. My people did not take the white girls. From what you have told me, I know a man and five of his followers that were once Chiricahua Apache did this thing. These men are no longer Chokonem Chiricahua Apache. They have been banished from among us. They now ride with the Comanchero."

"What is this man's name?" Jedidiah asked.

"He is called Nantaje."

"Where can I find him?"

"The Comanchero have a camp on the river, your people call, Rio Hondo, in the El Capitan Mountains. It would not be a wise thing for you to go. The Medal of Life will not protect you there."

"I've been called lots of things," Jedidiah told him. "Wise never was one of them. Am I free to go?"

"You should remain in our village a few days to renew your strength but you are free to go whenever you choose. You will be safe as long as you wear the medal. In return, I would ask your word of honor that you will never reveal the location of our camp."

"You have my word." Jedidiah promised, looking the Apache leader in the eyes. "I will never speak of it. All I have heard said of you, I have found to be true. You are a man of truth and honor. Thank you."

"Go in peace," Cochise said, rising to his feet. "Your horses and weapons will be waiting for you when you choose to leave."

Jedidiah lingered in the Apache village two more days. At first light on the third day he climbed stiffly into the saddle of his pinto. His pack mule, with all of his supplies intact, and weapons were returned to him just as Cochise had promised. He dug out his boots and stomped them on. They would be better for riding than the new moccasins the Indian women had provided. Even his Stetson was returned.

One of the older warriors was sent to lead him from the camp. To his amazement, the only visible entrance to the hidden valley was through a narrow, winding cave. Sometime in the distant past a stream had eaten an opening in the mountain, then dried up, leaving a long trail through the cave that opened into a blind canyon.

Nature had hidden the entrance to the cave with a waterfall. A mountain stream hurtled from a high ledge and plunged into the canyon below, then wound its way along the canyon floor. The only way through the falls, was through the falls. The pounding water soaked horse and rider.

It was a perfect hideout, one that would never be found unless someone had knowledge of the secret entrance. Once they passed through the opening, the narrow trail followed the stream as it wound along the canyon floor, finally opening like a huge funnel into a rocky valley.

Riding along behind the old warrior, a movement off to his left caught Jedidiah's eye. He swung a quick gaze.

He burst from among the rocks, mouth open, tongue lolling, tail wagging—Dog. Jedidiah reined up and swung quickly from his saddle. He knelt and opened his arms as his companion hurtled forward. Man and dog had a happy reunion.

"I knew you'd wait for me," Jedidiah told his friend. "It's good to see you big fellow, real good."

When they arrived back at the place where he had been taken captive, his Apache guide pulled up and raised his hand in the universal sign of peace. Jedidiah returned the goodbye as the old veteran of many battles reined his pony back up the trail and disappeared.

Chapter Nine

He was a tired and bone-weary rider that splashed across the Rio Grande River and climbed the steep incline toward Hobbs station. Already weakened, the long trek over the mountains and across two deserts had taken its toll on Jedidiah. All he wanted was a bed and about a week's rest. He decided he could go no further. He would spend a few days at the trading post resting up before setting out to find the Comanchero camp.

A half dozen barking hounds and twice that many curious children greeted him as he reined up in front of the post. Amos Hobbs, with his ever-present shotgun, lifted a hand in greeting.

"Never reckoned I'd see you again," his bullfrog voice boomed out.

"I wondered a time or two, myself," Jedidiah said, climbing wearily to the ground.

"Glad I's wrong."

"Me too."

"There's coffee. Mite old, but still drinkable."

"Sounds mighty good to me," Jedidiah said, loosening his saddle cinch.

"I got news you'll be wanting to hear," Hobbs said, spitting a stream of tobacco and watching it raise a puff of dust on the ground. "Don't know if it's good or bad."

"What kind of news?" Jedidiah asked, concern pulling his eyebrows together.

"Come on in and I'll tell it over coffee. You look a mite trail worn."

"Feel it, too."

Jedidiah stooped to get through the low door and slumped onto a rough bench beside a plank table. The old trapper's squaw poured a tin cup full of a thick, black liquid that resembled coffee. He chanced a sip. It was bitter and near chewable, but he swallowed it down and pretended it was good.

"Apache rode in a few days after you left. He never said a word, just tossed me a leather pouch and rode off."

Having said that, the trader paused and sipped from his coffee like that was the extent of the news. Jedidiah waited a long minute, impatient to hear the rest of it. The trader rubbed his scruffy beard for a long minute.

"In the pouch was a little girl's sleeping gown and a handful of hair. There was a note saying they wanted $50,000 thousand in gold brought to the old Gran Quivira mission by October 15."

"What's today?" Jedidiah asked anxiously.

"Don't ask me. I don't keep count," Hobbs told him.

"Where's the pouch?"

"I sent it to the Wells Fargo office in Sante Fe. Figured since I wouldn't see you no more that would be the best place."

"I've got to go," Jedidiah said, pushing wearily from the bench.

"None of my business," Hobbs offered, "but you ain't in no shape to go nowhere. You best rest up a spell."

"I'm afraid there ain't time," Jedidiah said, tramping from the room.

The trapper followed him outside. Jedidiah cinched his saddle, turned a stirrup, and pulled himself up. He half-hitched the lead to Mule, reined Butternut around, and heeled him into a short lope.

"I'm obliged for your help," he called over a shoulder.

Amos Hobbs shook his head and lifted a hand as Jedidiah rode away.

The sun had burned itself out and rested for the day. Dusk had settled and darkness was slowly spreading its black shroud over Sante Fe as a trail weary horse and rider plodded into town. Both the rider and his animals were covered with layers of grimy trail dust and sweat. Yellow patches of light from coal oil lamps made checkerboard squares along the dusty street. Saddled horses stood hipshot in front of three saloons being serenaded by strains from a rinky-tink piano that carried on a warm night. A light still showed in an upstairs window of the Wells Fargo office. Jedidiah reined up.

He unseated himself from the saddle and climbed wearily to the ground. The simple act of his boot encountering the ground jarred him to the very marrow of his bones. He let out a slow slide of air and looped Butternut's reins over the hitch rail.

"Stay, Dog," he said, the words coming out barely above a whisper.

The big wolf dog lay down in the thick dust underneath the pinto, his tired head rested on outstretched paws and its dark eyes followed Jedidiah as he stepped onto the boardwalk.

He knocked loudly on the door, waited, and knocked again. After the third try the door swung open. The surprised look was replaced by a huge grin that occupied most of Winston Taylor's face.

"Jedidiah Boone, you son-of-a-gun!" his friend exclaimed, extending a hand.

Jedidiah took it. The strength of their greeting confirmed the warm friendship between the two men.

"Howdy, Winston. Sounds like we need to talk."

"You've already heard. Come on in, Mr. Fargo is upstairs. You just don't know how glad we are to see you."

"Will it wait long enough for me to wash some of the trail off and grab a bite to eat? I've been riding hell-bent-for-leather ever since Amos Hobbs told me and a week before that."

"You go ahead and wash up. I'll have the restaurant bring over supper. We haven't eaten either. We can talk over a big steak. How's that sound?"

"Like sweet music, Winston, sweet music. I'll be back in an hour."

Taking up his reins, he decided, as tired as he was it'd be easier to walk the distance to the livery than it would to climb back into the saddle, besides, his legs had might near forgot how to work.

"Buenas Noches, señor," the old liveryman greeted as Jedidiah trudged up.

"Buenas Noches," Jedidiah said tiredly, handing him the reins. "Treat 'em good. They're plumb tuckered out. Double grain, rub 'em down and stall 'em. Dog will bed down in the stall too, but don't feed him."

"Si, señor."

Jedidiah draped his saddlebags over a shoulder and turned up the street. His spurs rattled in the stillness of the night as he walked along the boardwalk toward the Grand Hotel. He pushed through the front door. The desk clerk glanced up from a ledger and then stood as recognition crossed his face.

"Good evening, Mr. Boone."

"Howdy. I'll need a room and a bath."

"Yes, sir. Here's the key to number two, it's right down the hall. I'll have Juanitta prepare your bath right away."

"Just ask her to hurry it up. I ain't got much time."

"Right away, sir. I'll get right on it."

Jedidiah strode to his room. He pushed inside and tossed his saddlebags on the bed. It sure looks good. I ain't slept in a bed since I was here last time. He removed the globe from the coal oil lamp and struck a match on his britches leg. Flopping down on the bed he stretched out, knowing he had a few minutes before his bath would be ready.

His mind whirled. Will Mr. Fargo pay the ransom? Even if he does, will the kidnappers return the girls? Not likely. They'll most likely take the money and kill the girls anyway, or worse, sell them into prostitution in Mexico. If Mr. Fargo asks my opinion, what should I recommend they do? I'll have to give that some thought.

Reckon what Julianna is doing? Wonder if they've started their house yet? With any luck, and Mose and Minnie's help, they ought to get it built pretty quick.

Julianna...It makes my heart do flip-flops just to think about her.

A soft tap on the door jerked him back to reality.

"Who is it?" he called out.

"It is Juanitta, señor. I have your bath ready for you."

"I'll be right along," he called, pushing from the bed with great effort.

Glancing down at the buckskins the Apaches had given him he wrinkled his nose. Mingled sweat and trail dust clung heavily to the garments. He tried in vain to brush the dirt away. I'll ask Juanitta if she can do something with them while I'm in the bath, he decided.

Juanitta was waiting when he arrived at the bath stalls behind the hotel.

"Buenas Noches, señor Boone. It is good to see you again."

"Thank you," he replied, stepping inside the curtained booth. "I was wondering if you might brush up my buckskins while I'm in the tub? All my other clothes are dirty and I've got a meeting in an hour."

"Si. I will do my best. If you wish, I will be happy to wash your other clothes for you. I could have them clean and ready for you by noon tomorrow."

"That would be good," he told her. "I'll just be a minute getting in the tub and you can have my buckskins."

He soaked for the best part of a half hour, scrubbing himself with the bar of soap and the stiff brush he found beside the tub. He lay back and let the steaming water soothe his tired muscles.

Juanitta slid open the curtain and stepped inside with his cleaned buckskins.

"They are not clean, señor, but they are better than before."

"That's fine, Juanitta, I'm obliged," he said, slipping lower in the soapy water and reaching an arm to hand her a half-eagle. "I'll leave my other dirty clothes outside my door."

"Muchas Gracias, señor," she said, smiling and stepping out of the booth.

Jedidiah climbed the stairs at the Wells Fargo office wearily. Winston and Mr. Fargo were sitting at a table with a white cloth covering. They both pushed to their feet and greeted him warmly when he entered the large office.

"It's good to see you again, Mr. Boone," the Wells Fargo executive said, shaking his hand. "We were beginning to worry"

"It's good to be back," he told them, shaking hands with Winston.

"Have a seat," Winston said, motioning to a chair at the table." I'll go tell Rosetta we're ready to eat. I'll be right back."

"You've already heard about the ransom note, I understand," Fargo said, picking up a paper from his desk and passing it to Jedidiah.

He took the note and read it slowly and carefully, then reread it again, reading between the lines, considering not only what it said, but also what it didn't say.

"It says to deliver the money on the fifteenth. What's today?" Jedidiah asked.

"Today is the thirteenth," Fargo told him. "Winston says it will take a full days ride to get there. You'll have to leave in the morning."

"Then I take it you aim to pay them and you want me to deliver the money?"

"Why, yes. There was never any question. Like I said before, I'll do anything to get my nieces back unharmed."

"I could be wrong," Jedidiah told him, "but I don't think the two necessarily go together."

Winston walked in carrying a big tray piled high with food. A heavy-set Mexican woman followed him with another. They set the trays on the table. One of them held a silver coffeepot and cups. The woman poured three cups, then began setting the table.

"What..." Fargo started to speak, but stopped when Jedidiah crossed his lips with a finger in a sign for silence. The businessman nodded understanding.

They waited until the woman had finished and they heard the downstairs door close before continuing the conversation.

"The Comanchero may have big ears," Jedidiah explained. "

"Yes, of course. I didn't think," Fargo said. "What do you mean? Are you saying they may not release the girls even though we pay the ransom?"

"Mr. Fargo, you're a businessman. You're used to men doing what they say they'll do. I'm saying the men that took those little girls ain't that kind of men. After they get the money, they've got everything to lose and nothing to gain by giving the girls back. Think about it. The way I read the note, they're demanding two things. Notice the very first thing they asked for is that you drop out of the bidding on the government mail contract. I'm saying that's the most important thing to them. If it weren't, they'd have asked for the money first. Then they demanded fifty thousand in gold double-eagles.

"If they return the girls after you pay the ransom, what assurance do they have that you'll go along with the main thing they're after? They're sure not gonna take your word for it. No, I think when somebody shows up with all that money, they're planning on just taking it and keeping the girls to make sure you give up on that contract. That's why they want just one man to bring the money."

"Then are you suggesting I not pay them?"

"No sir, not exactly. I've been thinking on it. Let me tell you what I've got in mind and then you can decide."

Over supper he laid out his plan. They had all finished the thick, juicy steaks with all the trimmings by the time Jedidiah stopped talking, the longest string of words he'd put end-to-end since he could remember. Winston poured them all another cup of coffee.

Mr. Fargo took his cup and strode over to the window. For a long time he was quiet. He sipped his coffee and stared out the window into the night. Jedidiah and Winston waited.

"You say you believe the girls are being held in this Comanchero camp," Fargo asked, still staring out the window. "How do you know where this camp is?"

"Cochise told me," Jedidiah said.

"What?" Fargo exclaimed, spinning around. "You actually talked to the Apache chief? He told you where the Comanchero camp is?"

"Yes, sir."

"How did you manage that and still come back with your scalp?" Winston wanted to know.

"Just barely," Jedidiah told them. "It's a long story, I'll fill you in later. The Comanchero camp is on the Rio Hondo River in the El Capitan Mountains. That's south of here. It's less than a day's ride from the old mission where we're supposed to take the money.

"A renegade Apache named Nantaje and a half dozen of his men are the ones that killed your brother and took the girls. Cochise banished him and his followers from the tribe. They ride with the Comanchero now. But if you'll read the note real close, it wasn't any of them that wrote it.

"I reckon you've already figured out the fellow that's behind all this is someone who knows you, someone who's wanting that mail contract awfully bad."

"Yes, we know," Fargo nodded his head in agreement. "Winston and I have gone over every possibility of who it might be. We've got a few ideas, but no proof. I can't imagine who would do something like this just to win a contract."

Winston Taylor spoke up. "Jedidiah, you said awhile ago your whole plan hinged on eliminating whoever came to pick up the ransom money before they could harm the girls. What if they send a large group? Do you think you can get them all? What if they don't bring the girls? What if they leave them back at their camp, saying they'll release them later, what then?"

"I reckon it all comes down to this," Jedidiah told them. "Do you want to hand the money over and trust men like that to keep their word? Or do you want to trust me to get them all and do my dead level best to rescue the girls?"

Having had his say, Jedidiah sipped his coffee. Winston Taylor leaned back in his chair and looked at his boss. Mr. Fargo puffed on his big cigar and stared off at nothing for a long space of time.

Finally he spoke. "We'll do it your way."

The four girls waited. Dread gripped them, held them in its clutches. Elizabeth's chest tightened. She battled for every breath. Her ears rang with the roar of mounting panic. They're coming for us.

The bar was lifted. The door swung open. A big, filthy Mexican with tobacco streaked whiskers stepped inside. He swept the room with a quick glance. His eyes settled on Christine and Rosa.

In his own language he spat out a command. Elizabeth couldn't understand the words but the meaning was clear. They were taking the girls with them. Christine flicked a look of panic at Elizabeth. What can I do? How can I help my new friends? She pushed to her knees to plead for them.

"Please," she begged. "Please don't take them. Please don't hurt them any more."

Her words fell on deaf ears. The big Mexican's booted foot lashed out, the vicious kick burying into Elizabeth's side, sending her slamming into the wall. She saw exploding lights against a black background. Her ears rang...her side hurt...Rebecca screamed.

After a minute she gathered herself and crawled to the crack in the door. Christine and Rosa were hoisted into the same saddle.

Their feet were tied to the stirrup leather. One of the Mexicans took up the reins to the girl's horse. All four men mounted and rode away. Maybe they're taking them back home, she thought, but knew better.

Elizabeth and Rebecca were both still crying for their friends when Two Deers Running came to bring their daily ration of food and water.

"Where did they take our friends?" Elizabeth asked anxiously. "What are they going to do to them?"

A look of sadness crept across the Indian woman's face.

"They will be sold in Mexico," she said, lowering her eyes in shame. "You forget them. You never see them again."

"No...I won't forget them, Elizabeth's mind screamed. I may never see them again, but I will never forget them.

Jedidiah rode out at first light. Dog trotted along beside him. Behind him, a packhorse trailed on a long lead beside Mule. On the packhorse were strapped two metal strongboxes. In the boxes were twenty five hundred shiny new gold double-eagles, fifty thousand dollars.

That was by far more money than he had ever seen before. He had no intention of letting anybody ride off into the sunset with it, at least as long as he was able to stop them. Mr. Fargo trusted him and he would do everything in his power not to let him down.

He twisted in the saddle to gaze back over his shoulder. Winston Taylor was there, standing on the boardwalk in front of the Wells Fargo office. His friend waved. Jedidiah lifted a hand. His face tightened. His thoughts galloped ahead. Can I do what I've set out to do? What if the whole Comanchero band is there? I can't possibly kill them all. What if I fail? They'll get the gold and kill the girls too. I can't let that happen! I won't let that happen!

* * *

The old Gran Quivira mission was one of four locations that made up a group called the Salinas Pueblo missions. Established early in the seventeenth century by Spanish Franciscans, they were abandoned in failure less than fifty years later when a great drought ravaged the area, causing the Pueblo to move farther west. Now it was nothing but ruins, a series of high rock walls that formed a maze of roofless rooms. Jedidiah had passed the ruins several times before during his scouting expeditions. A little spring fed stream of good water made it a welcome stopover for many thirsty travelers.

A good night's sleep had helped but he was still tired. He relaxed against the cantle of his saddle and let his body adjust to the gentle rocking motion of Butternut's easy gait. He had plenty of time. The rendezvous wasn't until sundown of the following day, but he wanted to get there early and look the place over closer.

The sun peeked over the distant horizon and was welcomed by a clear, blue, cloudless sky. He liked to watch the sunrise. He often sat in his old rocking chair on the front porch of his cabin with a hot cup of coffee and watched the birth of a new day. The world seemed fresh and clean in the early morning.

Knotting the reins around his saddle horn, he took out the makings and rolled himself a quirley. Striking a match on the leg of his buckskin, he put fire to it and took a long inhale. The harsh sweetness of the smoke settled inside him. He held it for a long moment and let it out in a slow slide. A relaxing feeling crept through his body. He rode on.

It was good dark when he saw the outline of the old ruins up ahead against a starlit sky. His searching gaze swept the area for signs of life but saw none. He reined up. Dog's head lifted to look at him.

"Better take a look around, Dog," he said.

Jedidiah swept an arm up, arching it in the direction of the abandoned mission. The wolfdog responded immediately, wheeling and trotted forward, and was quickly swallowed up by the darkness. Jedidiah sat his saddle. Long minutes passed before Dog returned with his tail wagging. No one was around.

The old mission was built on three levels. Jedidiah chose the highest and found a square, rock enclosure that gave him a clear view of the surrounding area. It opened through a door onto a large courtyard that faced the direction from which he expected the Comanchero to come. For what he had in mind, it would do just fine.

He led his three animals into an adjoining room and strung a rope line across the width and tied his animals to it. He unsaddled all three, then led them to the nearby stream so they could slake their thirst.

Rustling up wood from dead mesquite trees, he built a small fire and put on a pot of coffee. While it was heating he cut some salt bacon into a frying pan and sliced in a couple of potatoes. He hadn't eaten since his supper with Winston and Mr. Fargo the night before.

He ate slowly and enjoyed the relaxed meal. Afterward, he poured a second cup of coffee into his tin cup and leaned his back against the rock wall of the old ruins. Dog lay beside him, his muzzle resting on his outstretched paws.

A myriad of stars dotted a velvety, dark sky. A full moon inched along its journey and lit the night near bright as day...a full moon...a Comanche moon...a moon made for lovers, Julianna had said.

The campfire licked into the air, casting a jagged circle of light in the rock-enclosed room. Two hundred years ago people lived here, he thought. Most likely a man and his woman sat right where I'm sitting...talked about the future...made love...raised a family...and maybe died. Maybe two hundred years from now somebody else will sit right here where I'm sitting...and I'll be part of the past.

By the time the coffeepot was dry and the fire nothing but a glowing pile of hot coals, Jedidiah's eyelids got in the way of his seeing. He checked the load on both of his .12 gauge sawed-off double barrel shotguns, scooted down into his bedroll, and quickly dropped into a sound sleep.

Julianna couldn't sleep. She'd lain awake for hours, trying to be quiet so as not to wake her mother. Finally, she slipped quietly from the bed they shared in one of the covered wagons and eased carefully down the familiar four steps to the ground. Pulling the wrap tightly around her shoulders, she padded barefooted to the nearby campfire. Using an iron poker, she stoked the fire to life and added several sticks. Sitting down on one of the big logs that surrounded the fire, she stared into the flames as they leaped higher and higher. The campfire swabbed the night with a soft glow, then melded into darkness only a few feet away.

It was a cool fall night, somewhere around the middle of October, though she wasn't exactly sure of the date. Mose had said the snows would start soon. She sure hoped they had the cabin finished before then.

The thought of their cabin caused her to lift her gaze to assure herself it was still there, that it wasn't just a figment of her imagination. It was going to be a glorious home, far more than what either she or her mother had even dared dream for. Mose had turned out to be quite a builder and with everyone working from dawn until dusk, the walls were all up and they were now putting the roof on. Papa said they should be able to move in within a week. What a day that would be, to actually live in a house again.

The whole family had fallen in love with Mose and Minnie. They were both so strong, and yet so gentle. Julianna had engaged Minnie in conversation several times about Jedidiah, questioning her about his background...what he was like, and all.

"I swear to my time, girl," Minnie had said after the second conversation. "I do believe you be sweet on that man."

"I do believe you're right," she had answered unashamedly and they shared a laugh. Since then, they had become the best of friends.

Lost in quiet reverie, Julianna lifted her face to stare up at a clear sky. It was a beautiful night...a perfect night. A full moon bathed the night in a muted softness...a full moon...what had Jedidiah called it?...Oh yes, he had called it a Comanche moon...A lovers moon. Wonder where he is tonight?...Wonder if he might possibly be looking up at the moon...and thinking of me. The thought brought an immediate feeling of closeness, as if they shared a mutual bond.

Twinkling stars littered the dark sky like flakes of gold sprinkled across a sea of purest indigo. Her gaze focused on the brightest of them. A little child's poem she had taught her class back in Missouri came to mind. "Starlight, star bright, first star I've seen tonight. Wish I may, wish I might, have the wish I wish tonight."

If I could have just one wish, what would it be? That's easy...She closed her eyes. A flushed feeling crept over her. Her heart swelled inside her chest. Tears were born and escaped her shuttered eyes and scored hot trails down her cheeks. Her lips moved in a silent plea...I wish Jedidiah would return safely to me. At the thought, emotion welled within her, a lump rose in her throat. Surely no one has a right to be this happy! She thought. But incredible as it seemed to her, she was.

Again closing her misty-green eyes, she sighed deeply with contentment. Her skin, misted with the damp night air, glistened in the low light from the campfire. Her long golden hair, unbound, rippled like shocks of ripe wheat with each gust of a cool, whispering breeze.

At the very thought of Jedidiah, a wave of tiny tremors shook her, and then another. They began deep in her core and pulsed through her body like ripples along the top of a pool of water.

A quiet sound behind her scattered her thoughts.

"What are you doing out here by yourself, honey?" her mother asked, sitting down beside her on the log and wrapping half the blanket she held around Julianna's shoulders. "You'll catch a death of cold."

"Oh mother, I'm so worried about Jedidiah," she said, wiping the tears from her face with the edge of the blanket. "What if something bad happens to him? I don't think I could stand it."

"I know how you feel, honey. There wasn't a night while your father was gone to war that I didn't feel what you're feeling right now. I guess that's a woman's lot, to worry about her man."

"I love him, mother. I never dreamed I could feel about someone like I do about him. I know we haven't had much time together, but how much time does it take to fall in love?"

"Just one heartbeat, honey...Just one heartbeat."

They sat together for a long time, mother and daughter. Snuggled together under the blanket against the chill of early morning, watching the fire. It was one of those times one never forgets, one of those memories that last a lifetime.

Morning came slow. Elizabeth had slept little. Thankfully, her sister was still asleep. Taking up her sharp rock, Elizabeth scratched the sixty-second mark on the wall. It had been two days since the Comanchero came and took Christine and Rosa away. Both Elizabeth and Rebecca were devastated at the loss of their friends and went on a two day crying spree. They clung to each other for comfort, cried themselves to sleep, and then roused to weep again.

Rebecca didn't understand. She kept asking where the bad men had taken their friends? How could she explain? She groped for words to reassure her little sister but found none. After Rebecca would finally cry herself to sleep, Elizabeth huddled on her own blanket with her face in her hands. Tears drizzled hot and salty between her fingers.

As she did daily, she crawled over to the door and peered through the crack. There was activity in the camp. Men were scurrying about, saddling horses, going in and out of the scattered adobe shacks. Something was going on.

As she watched, they began to gather down by the river. They watered their horses and milled about, waiting for something. Nantaje and the five Indians that usually rode with him were there. She counted three others that looked like Americans and two Mexicans. All of them looked like mean men. Their clothes were dirty and they wore heavy beards. Most of them wore ammunition belts that crisscrossed their chests. All of them wore at least one pistol, some two.

Across the river, She saw the one called Scarface come out of his house. He swung easily onto his black horse's bare back and splashed across the water to join the others. It was obvious they were getting ready to go somewhere.

A feeling of excitement surged through her. Maybe Two Deers Running would let them bathe in the river again like she did before. Elizabeth remembered how good the cold water felt, how good it felt to be clean. She thought about waking Rebecca and telling her the good news. Then her thoughts were shattered. Two of the Americans turned and started up the hill leading three horses.

Elizabeth gasped. Fear blossomed in her chest and a cry pushed up her throat. They're coming for us! They're taking us to Mexico! They're going to sell us like they did Christine and Rosa. No one will ever see us again.

She scrambled over and shook Rebecca awake...gathering her little sister in her arms...holding her tight. Rebecca sensed Elizabeth's alarm and mumbled against her chest.

"What is it...what's wrong, sis?"

Before she could answer the door swung open. Both girls screamed. A bearded giant grabbed each of them by an arm and dragged them outside kicking and screaming. Elizabeth pounded the man with her free fist. He ignored her thrashing and lifted them both into the same saddle.

"This one's a regular little wildcat," he told the other man. "I like 'em like that. To bad the boss won't let me give her a go. She's a real looker."

"Yeah," the other one replied, spitting an ugly stream of tobacco juice. "She'd be more fun than that little Mex gal. She didn't have no spunk about her a-tall."

Both girl's hands were bound and their feet were quickly secured to the stirrup straps. A strip of rag was tied tightly around their mouth, muffling their screams. One of the men took up the reins to the horse the two girls were on. Both Comanchero mounted, and together, rejoined the others as they all rode out of camp.

Chapter Ten

Jedidiah spent the day preparing, playing out the upcoming battle in his mind. He checked and rechecked his weapons, loading them to capacity. Winston had provided a second sawed-off, twelve gauge shotgun. He loaded both of them and laid them on a protruding rock just inside the opening that led to the courtyard. Beside them, he hung an ammunition belt filled with double-ought shells. The shotguns would be his first method of assault.

A few feet from the door opening, he used his Bowie to loose a shoulder-high rock and remove it from the ancient wall. It provided an ideal gun port. He fed fifteen .44-40 cartridges into his Henry rifle and canted it against the wall. He dug the extra pistol from his saddlebag and loaded both of the Frontier model .44's. One he returned to its holster, the other he jammed down the waistband of his britches.

Taking another long look around, he tried to anticipate how it would all play out, and considered everything he could think of that might not go according to the plans he had laid out. Finally deciding he had done everything possible to prepare for every eventuality, he felt he was ready. All three horses were saddled and waiting. The two strongboxes containing the gold coins were strapped securely to the packhorse. All he could do now was wait

He spent the next hour exploring the maze of connecting rooms that made up the venerable Mission. He was amazed at the complexity of the design and workmanship. The interconnecting and multiple level structure had withstood the harshness of weather and time for more than two hundred years. Undoubtedly, many battles had been fought here. Today, there would be one more, perhaps his last.

As the sun dipped near the western horizon, he pulled his long, linen duster around him and slouched down to sit with his back against the rock wall. He fished the makings from a shirt pocket and rolled himself a smoke. He had to cup his hand against a hot east wind to light his cigarette. Dog lay down beside him. Jedidiah leaned his head back against the wall, inhaled a long puff, and stared blankly at the fading sunset.

A gust of hot wind swirled powdery dust around him, blowing grit into his eyes. He blinked it away and watched a desert hawk soaring a circle above him. The hawk screeched a cry that was lost in the wind. I guess I'm as ready as I'm ever going to be, he thought, taking a deep breath and blowing it out.

The blistering sun sank lower, drowning itself in a blood-colored blaze and framing the faraway horizon that was silhouetted against the fiery sky. That's when he saw the dust. It rose in a boiling cloud and was quickly scattered by the wind.

At first they appeared as a mere black speck in the shimmering haze of heat waves. The speck became a fuzzy outline of horsemen that appeared to dance above the desert. With a hand, Jedidiah shielded his eyes from the sun and waited. One thing he was already sure of, the odds weren't going to be good.

He snubbed the cigarette stub in the sand and pushed to his feet. Turning, he walked the few steps to stand in the door opening of the rock wall. His right hand lifted the .44 Colt and let it settle comfortably back in its holster. With the curl of a finger he swept his duster open and tucked it behind the butt of his pistol. Reaching a hand, he tilted the wide-brimmed Stetson to shield his eyes from the setting sun.

"Back, Dog," Jedidiah spoke, lifting a hand to wave the wolfdog out of sight inside the structure.

I count twelve, he thought. Pretty stiff odds, but I'll play the hand dealt me.

They rode straight in. Jedidiah picked out the leader while they were still three hundred yards off. One would have to have been blind to miss him. He sat straight and tall on the bare back of a big, high stepping, coal-black stallion. He had that easily identifiable characteristic of leadership about him.

They rode into the courtyard and reined up, scattering out in a ragged line. Jedidiah spotted the girls on his far left. The reins to their horse were held by a big, dirty looking American—he'd have to be among the first to die, Jedidiah decided.

Were it not for the long scar that marred his tanned face, the leader could have been called handsome. Tall and square-shouldered, lean and well muscled. His long, dark hair was held in place by a red bandanna, the mark of an Apache warrior. This was the half-breed they called Scarface...the scourge of the desert...the ghostlike leader of the Comanchero.

Scarface sat his horse. For a long minute they stared at each other. Then his dark, flashing eyes flicked about, sweeping the whole area in a searching gaze.

"You came alone," the man said, a statement instead of a question. He spoke perfect English, his voice clear and powerful, "I didn't think you would."

"You didn't come alone," Jedidiah replied.

The man stared at Jedidiah for a long moment. They were the eyes Jedidiah would have imagined the devil himself might possess. Then his lips curled in an easy smile.

"You really didn't think I would, did you?"

"Nope."

"Who are you?"

"Who I am ain't important. Why I'm here, is."

"Did you bring the gold?"

"Why else would I come?"

"You can see the girls. You have seen them. I need to see the gold."

Jedidiah backed up through the door opening, his gaze never leaving the riders. Reaching a hand, he took up the reins of the packhorse and moved it a few steps to stand just inside the doorway. Lifting the lid to one of the strongboxes, he scooped a fistful of the double-eagles and flung them at the feet of the leader's prancing black stallion. The shiny new gold coins captured the last rays of a setting sun and glittered against the white sand.

"Send the packhorse forward," Scarface ordered. "Then I will release the girls."

"I'm just supposed to take your word for that? I don't think so. When the girl's horse is inside this doorway, then you can have the gold."

"We could just kill you and take the gold and the girls too," the Comanchero leader said. "They would bring a high price in Mexico, beside, my men are itching to have a little fun before we sell them."

Jedidiah knuckled his mustache with a left hand, Then tugged at his earlobe for a brief moment, considering the man's words. His right thumb remained hooked in his gunbelt.

"I reckon you could try."

Jedidiah felt his body tense. He watched the leader closely, alert for any signal, any move to draw his weapon. For a slice of eternity measured only in seconds, they waited. A horse snorted. The leader's high-spirited stallion pranced in place, tossing its big head, eyes wide, nostrils flaring.

"You are a brave man...a stupid one...but brave," Scarface finally said. Then without altering his stare from Jedidiah, gave an order. "Give him the girls."

The big American holding the girl's horse nudged his mount forward. He walked his red sorrel up to the doorway. Out of the corner of his eye, Jedidiah saw the man hesitate. The Comanchero pinned Jedidiah with a cold stare, then handed him the reins.

While the American turned his horse to return to his compadres, Jedidiah guided the girl's horse through the door and into the room enclosure, still keeping his gaze fixed on the leader.

His hand slapped the girl's horse on the rump, moving it well inside the room. His left hand remained hidden behind the wall just long enough to close on the stock of the sawed-off, double-barreled shotgun.

With his right hand, he reached as if to place it against the right side of the door opening, instead, it grasped the second shotgun lying on the protruding rock. Jedidiah's features went stony. He glanced down, studying the ground for a long moment. When his eyes lifted, his mouth was set in a tight line.

"On the other hand," Jedidiah said, his voice suddenly cold and hard. "I could just kill you and take it all."

The final word hadn't left his mouth when both hands suddenly appeared, each holding a cocked shotgun. The Comanchero leader's eyes rounded. A shocked look distorted his face as the first two barrels exploded.

At twenty feet, the damage inflected by the heavy double-ought shot upon man and beast was devastating. Men cursed and died with the screams still on their lips. Horses whinnied shrilly and reared. And the silence of the desert dusk was transformed into the sound of death.

Heavy blue smoke from the twin blasts clouded around him, stinging his nose with its acrid stench. He squinted and peered through the hazy curtain of gunsmoke. Disregarding the horses that were down or falling, he concentrated on those riders still in the saddle and swung the noses of the shotguns there.

A wad of confused riders fighting frightened mounts caught his eye. He swung the nose of a shotgun and feathered the trigger. The gun bucked and roared, sending shock waves up Jedidiah's arm. Blood and bone fragments splayed into the air. Men screamed and clutched at torn faces, their hands leaking fountains of red between their fingers. Horses went down to their knees, threshing about.

Two riders fought their horses to turn them about. Jedidiah swung the right hand shotgun and triggered it off. One Comanchero flew from his saddle, arms and legs wind-milling the air as if he had sprouted wings. The second rider arched his back when the pellets tore into him, then slumped forward and toppled from his saddle.

The coppery scent of blood reached Jedidiah's nostrils on a rush of hot wind. Wheeling, he dove through the door opening as several slugs ricocheted off the rock wall and whined off into the fading light. Scrambling to his feet, he dropped the shotguns at his feet and snatched up the Henry rifle. Poking its nose through the hole in the wall he had made, he searched for a target.

An Apache heeled his horse forward, charging for the opening in the wall. Jedidiah centered the man's chest and fired. The force of the .44 slug at close range blew the Indian from his saddle, doing a backward somersault from his pony. His body bounced when it hit the sand, his legs twitching in death spasms.

The battleground was littered with dead and dying horses and men. Some still fought their animals, trying desperately to turn them to flee. Others abandoned their mounts, scrambling on foot for cover.

Jedidiah fired, levered, and fired again and again and again. It was hard to miss at such a close range. Bullets bit into the wall around his porthole. Still he found target after target and kept firing.

Jedidiah's eyes burned from the gunsmoke. His face was drenched with beads of sweat. His rifle grew hot in his hands before snapping on an empty chamber. A sound from behind him reached his hearing. He wheeled toward the sound. An Apache appeared in the doorway from an adjoining room. He held a rifle waist-high and leveled at Jedidiah.

Twisting on tiptoes, Jedidiah threw himself sideways. A finger of bright flame blossomed from the nose of the Indian's rifle even as Jedidiah's .44 pistol leaped into his hand. The pistol barked twice. Two black holes poked through a bronze chest. Twin fountains of blood erupted, pumping out the man's life with every remaining heartbeat.

Two more Indians poured through the front opening. Before Jedidiah could swing around, Dog took two running bounds and leaped. His body hurtled through the air, fangs bared, lips snarling. The impact of his attack threw the Apaches off balance. One went down under the weight of the animal. He fought frantically, trying to ward off the lunging mouth from his throat. He failed. The steel, trap-like jaws slammed shut on the Indian's throat. The animal shook his head violently, as he would shake a rabbit. Within seconds the man stopped fighting and lay deathly still, his legs jerking in after-death reflexes.

Jedidiah shot the other Indian in the face. The heavy slug tore through a cheekbone and took half his head with it when it came out the back. He was dead before his body hit the sandy floor.

Casting quickly about, Jedidiah saw the packhorse carrying the strongboxes disappearing through the opening in the back of the room. The girl's horse was right behind him. Butternut and his pack mule were nowhere to be seen, obviously already having taken leave. He snatched up the two shotguns and ammunition belts and followed the girl's horse.

Inside the second room the four horses danced nervously. Jedidiah flattened his back against the wall and pressed one of the shotguns underneath an arm. He thumbed open the other. From one of the ammunition belts he fingered out two shells and nosed them into the dark chambers of the .12 gauge. Flipping a wrist, he slammed it shut, traded places with the remaining weapon, and repeated the process.

He had no idea how many of the enemy remained. He had been lucky. He had caught them completely by surprise and that had been his edge. One thing for sure, they weren't going to just give up and ride away from all that money.

A sound above him spun him around. An Apache warrior was just pushing off the top of the wall, diving headlong toward him. Jedidiah's right hand swung up. The sawed-off blasted. The angry pellets intercepted the attacker in mid-flight. Like a swarm of angry bees the heavy shot tore into him. Blood, chunks of flesh, and pulverized bone fragments showered into the air. What was left of his body fell in a heap at Jedidiah's feet.

From the other room, Jedidiah heard Dog. He could tell by the sound he was in a battle. Jedidiah stepped to the opening and peered around the wall.

Dog had an Apache treed. The frightened Indian was in one corner of the room with his back against the rock wall. His rifle lay nearby, just out of his reach. He was slashing with his knife, fighting the dog off. The big wolfdog dashed in, teeth bared, then retreated from the flashing blade only to lunge in again.

Jedidiah hated to spoil his companion's fun, but he didn't have time to enjoy the show. He tucked the shotgun from his right hand underneath his left arm. Withdrawing his .44, he raised it to eye level, took aim, and put a bullet right through the Apache's evil heart. His body slammed against the rock wall, then toppled facedown to the sandy floor, his right leg twitched in an after death spasm. Dog straddled the body, sniffed, then trotted to stand beside his master.

Moving swiftly, Jedidiah pressed against the wall near the front opening where the battle began. With shotguns in hand, he chanced a quick look around the edge of the wall at the courtyard.

It reminded him of another battlefield, one called Shiloh. Horses and men lay everywhere, some piled on top of others. A few were badly wounded. Their cries and screams filled the darkening sky. His gaze spotted no moving enemy. Hurrying back to the adjoining room, he pressed against the wall beside the door and waited.

After what seemed an eternity, his hearing picked up a single horse pounding away at a gallop. Someone was getting away. Still he waited.

He wanted to untie the girls, to hug them close, to comfort them and dry their tears and tell them they would soon be safely back with their uncle. But he knew that until the battle was over the best place for them was right where they were, so he waited some more.

Finally, he decided the enemy was all either dead, dying, or had slipped away in the darkness. Moving cautiously, he crept to the first room, then through the front opening into the courtyard. Light from a full moon, and a sky full of twinkling stars lit the courtyard and revealed the devastating scene. The screams ceased, the wounded had died.

Moving through the bloody mass of bodies that littered the battlefield Jedidiah counted...eleven. Only one had gotten away...Wonder which one?

Searching the area, he failed to find either Scarface or the prancing black stallion. The Comanchero leader had somehow managed to survive and get away. He was the one I heard riding away. That's bad news, Jedidiah thought. Of all the ones to get away, why did it have to be him?

Hurrying back inside, he quickly untied the girls and lifted them to the ground. The terror on their faces had been replaced with a look of confusion. They shied back from him, cringing, clutching each other close. Jedidiah saw the bruises on the older girl's face and a new anger swept over him. What kind of men would hurt innocent little girls like that?

"Don't be afraid," Jedidiah told them in a soft voice. "Your Uncle William Fargo sent me. I'm going to take you home. No one's gonna hurt you any more."

The smallest girl was still snubbing, her small body jerking with each sharp inhale. Jedidiah saw the older sister glance through the door at the bodies lying in the next room, then up at Jedidiah with questioning eyes.

"Did you...did you kill them all?"

"All but one. The leader got away, the one they call Scarface. But he won't bother you anymore. If you girls feel up to it, we'll ride a ways before we stop for the night. We should have you back home sometime tomorrow."

The afternoon sun was mid way along its downward path when Jedidiah and his little procession rode into Sante Fe. Somebody spotted them and shouted out the news. Excited townspeople took up the cry and within seconds, the whole town was buzzing with the news.

"The Fargo girls have been rescued!" somebody screamed excitedly. "The kidnapped girls are back safe!"

Word quickly reached William Fargo and Winston Taylor and they hurried down to the street.

Bedraggled and trail weary, their hair in tangles, and wearing dirty doeskin Indian dresses, the two girls slumped in their single saddle. Elizabeth held onto the saddle horn, Rebecca rode behind the saddle, her small arms encircling her big sister's waist.

Jedidiah reined up in front of the Wells Fargo office. He tossed the reins to the girl's horse and the lead rope to the packhorse carrying the two chests of gold to Winston.

William Fargo, his eyes brimming with tears, lifted the girls from their mount with gentle hands. Disregarding his lofty position and forgetting his impeccably pressed suit, he stood them on the ground and dropped to his knees in the dusty street. Gathering his nieces in his arms, he wept unashamedly.

Winston Taylor quickly untied the two strongboxes from the packhorse and, with the help of two workers from the Wells Fargo office, carried them inside.

"I'll see to the horses," Jedidiah told his friend. "I'll stop by the office after I've had myself a long bath."

"Why don't we all have supper together over at the Sante Fe restaurant if you feel up to it?" Winston asked.

"That'll allow time to get the girls cleaned up, too. I think this calls for a celebration."

Mr. Fargo overheard what was said and raised his reddened eyes without loosening his hug of the girls.

"I couldn't agree more," he said, his quivering voice betraying his emotions.

"We'll stop by the hotel around six and walk over together," Winston said.

"Sounds good to me," Jedidiah assured him, taking up the lead ropes to Mule and the unburdened packhorse. He reined Butternut around and headed for the livery stable.

He left his animals in the capable hands of the old holster, then headed for the hotel. After picking up the key to his room, he stepped out back and arranged for a hot bath. Juanitta told him the clothes he had left with her were cleaned and hanging in his room. She assured him the water was already hot and that his bath would be ready in minutes.

It was. He climbed gingerly into the steaming water and lowered himself slowly. Leaning back against the large wooden tub, he forced himself to close his eyes and relax. The hot water soaked into him, soothing his tired, aching muscles. His mind ground down to a slow spin. Maybe this ordeal is over and done with, he thought.

He hadn't even realized he had drifted off to sleep until voices woke him. He jerked his head up. His eyes snapped open. His hearing brought recognition of the voices. It was Elizabeth and Rebecca. They were in the next bath stall. Juanitta was helping them bathe.

"His name is, Jedidiah," Elizabeth's voice continued a conversation they obviously had already been having. "I think he works for my Uncle Fargo. He sure is a nice man."

"Yeah," chimed in her younger sister. "He killed all the bad men."

"Si," Juanitta said. "He is a very nice man. He is very handsome too."

"Uncle Fargo said we're all having a big celebration tonight, with a cake and everything."

"Si, your Uncle is picking out some brand new clothes for you at the store right now. They will be in your room when you are finished with your bath. He asked me to help you with your bath and hair. He wants you both to look beautiful tonight."

"The bad men killed our father and mother," Elizabeth told their new Mexican friend.

"I am very sad for you," Juanitta told them. "Your Uncle loves you very much. He will see that you are cared for. Come. We must hurry. We have much to do to get both of you beautiful for your celebration."

Jedidiah waited until they were gone before he climbed out of the tub. He dried, dressed, and headed for the barbershop. He wanted to get his ears lowered before supper.

They were all waiting for him in the lobby of the hotel when Jedidiah came down the stairs. He hardly recognized the girls. Both wore brand new clothes from head to toe. Rebecca looked like an angel in a white dress with pink ribbon interlaced along the hem and sleeves. Elizabeth wore a powder-blue dress with white lace. Their blonde hair was washed and brushed, and now hung like golden corn silk about their shoulders. Shiny ribbons crowned their heads.

"Well, now," Jedidiah said. "Someone will have to introduce me to these two beautiful young ladies. I don't reckon we've ever met."

"It's me, Mr. Jedidiah...Rebecca. Don't you remember?" she rebuked him.

"I remember a girl named, Rebecca," he said, a grin gathering and breaking across his face, "but she didn't look anything like this."

"They sure got all gussied up just to go to supper with three old men, didn't they?" Winston joshed.

"Are you all going to stand there gabbing all night? I, for one, am starving," Mr. Fargo told them, taking Rebecca's hand and heading for the door. "Come on honey, we'll get there first and get the best of everything. I've got a feeling they've got a great big cake waiting just for you."

It was a happy group that strolled from the hotel and started down the boardwalk toward the Sante Fe restaurant, all talking and laughing.

Elizabeth was walking beside Jedidiah, holding his hand. Suddenly he felt her hand tighten. A sharp gasp sounded from an indrawn breath. Alarm radiated through her touch. He could sense the girl's panic spiraling, smell the fear on her skin. She stopped dead in her tracks.

Jedidiah slanted a quick look at her. A mask of horror covered her face. She stared straight ahead, her eyes widened in fear. He swung his gaze to follow hers.

Three men had just emerged from the saloon. They huddled in intent conversation. Two of them were Hume and Honeycutt, the two Wells Fargo detectives that worked for Winston. The other was a short, chubby little fellow with tiny spectacles and a flushed, reddish face. He wore a black bowler hat.

"It's them!" Elizabeth said in a loud whisper, her voice fraying. "Those three men, they were at the camp where they held us!"

"What..." Mr. Fargo said. "You must be mistaken, dear. Two of those men are detectives. They work for Wells Fargo. The other man works for a prominent businessman."

"They were there, I tell you!" She said emphatically, lifting a frantic gaze to Jedidiah. "I saw them. The one with the glasses came to our room and looked at me. The tall one was riding a horse just like yours, Mr. Jedidiah's, a black and white pinto."

He could hear the certainty in Elizabeth's quavering voice. He could see the barely controlled panic in her young face.

"She's telling the truth," Jedidiah said. "There's no other way she could know Hume rides a pinto like mine."

"Oh, my God!" Winston exclaimed. "That would explain why Homer Douglas has been hanging around town. Why, it's as plain as the nose on your face! His boss, John Holladay's, the one behind all this."

"That might also explain the tracks I found at the Fargo ranch," Jedidiah told them. "Two of the raiders that slaughtered those folks rode shod horses."

Memories of the atrocities at the Fargo ranch gave birth to outrage. Outrage bled to anger and anger into action. Jedidiah's blue eyes narrowed and, cold as ice, fixed upon the three men. His eyes went smoky and a dark scowl settled over his face. Without diverting his gaze, he spoke to his friends in a low voice.

"Mr. Fargo," Jedidiah said. "Keep the girls back out of the way. Winston, go get the sheriff."

"What are you going to do?" Winston asked.

Jedidiah slowly knuckled his mustache and exchanged a look with his friend.

"I'm gonna read to them fellows from the book," Jedidiah said, sweeping the edge of his buckskin jacket behind the butt of his pistol.

His jaw set...his mouth razored in a thin line...his eyes again fixed in a hard stare. Striding forward with measured and determined steps, he didn't stop until he was within arm's reach of the three men.

Jedidiah reckoned Detective Hume to be the most dangerous, supposing himself to be some kind of gun slick. The detective had just lit a smoke and was inhaling his first drag. Jedidiah's left hand shot out in a blur, slapping the cigarette from the man's mouth with the back of his hand. Before the man could react, Jedidiah whipped out his Colt and clouted the agent across his forehead. He crumbled to the boardwalk.

"What the..."

His partner's question never got asked. Again the pistol lashed out, landing just above Detective Honeycutt's right ear, dropping him like a sack of potatoes.

Wheeling, the hand holding the Colt shot forward, Jedidiah's arm extended. The pistol's cold nose pressed just below the brim of the black Bowler hat in the very center of the pudgy little man's forehead. Behind his spectacles, eyes walled white. He drew in a gasp of air on a sharp inhale.

Jedidiah's eyes went cold and deadly, his voice low and menacing.

"I'm a man of little patience, mister," he said just above a whisper. "I'm gonna ask you a question. I'm only gonna ask it once. After I ask it, you got half a dozen heartbeats to give me a straight answer. If you lie to me, I'm gonna blow your brains all over the street. Do you understand?"

Great drops of sweat popped out on the man's forehead. He licked suddenly dry lips. He frantically nodded his head.

Winston Taylor and Sheriff Medlock arrived, guns drawn. They appraised the situation with a glance and stood silently nearby.

"Those two little girls over yonder tell me you was at the Comanchero camp. Is that true?"

Jedidiah thumbed back the hammer of his Colt. The metallic whir of the turning cylinder echoed in the stillness like a death knell.

The man's eyes showed panic, then despair. He slowly nodded his head.

"A nod just ain't good enough, mister," Jedidiah said, sensing the presence of the lawman standing nearby. "The sheriff here needs to hear you say it. Do it!"

The man's mouth quirked in a pitiful, quivering rasp.

"I was there," he blurted out, "but I had nothing to do with killing that family, honest. That was Hume and Honeycutt's idea. They said they had to make it look good. They said we had to put the scare in Fargo or he'd never fork over that much money."

"What about the other part?" Jedidiah asked. "Whose idea was it to demand Wells Fargo drop out of the bidding for the mail contract?"

"That wasn't me! It was my boss! All I done was write the ransom note. Mr. Holladay bought into the railroad and wanted to get the mail contract. He said if we could get Fargo to drop out, we'd be the only remaining bidder. I was just doing what he told me, I swear I was."

"I've heard enough," Sheriff Medlock said, bending to relieve the two unconscious detectives of their weapons. "These two will stretch a rope. It'll be up to a jury to decide what happens to Holladay and this weasel, but I suspect they'll be gone for a mighty long time."

Chapter Eleven

Julianna knew she was dreaming. Somewhere in the deepest recesses of her mind she knew it was only a dream. But how could it be? It felt so real.

Jedidiah was kissing her, softly, lingeringly, as though he intended to savor every honeyed moment of it. She was returning his kiss, eagerly opening her lips to him, her arms to him, wanting all he demanded, and more.

It's only a dream...but then why do I feel this fire deep inside me...flickering...building...blazing? Why are the hot chills dancing up and down my spine?

It's only a dream...a bold, beautiful dream born in my heart from the very first moment we met. But since it's only a dream, there's no need to hold my emotions in check. I need not refrain from kissing him and touching him, as I've wanted to do since the moment he took me in his arms.

But it's only a dream, I've wished it so hard, so many times, but if it's only a dream then let me dream on. I never want to wake.

Julianna awoke.

Streamers of light slanted through the window of her very own, brand new bedroom, spilling across her bed. She stretched luxuriantly and snuggled into her soft feather pillow, a blissful smile playing across her lips. Maybe today Jedidiah will come home. She had been making that secret wish to herself every morning for the last two weeks.

Outside, the sounds of morning reached her: Chirping birds could be heard above the now familiar, roar of Angel falls. She heard their cow bawl, begging to be milked. The bull answered with a loud bellow. From across the breezeway of their divided cabin, voices drifted to her, soft and muffled. The aroma of fresh boiled coffee tickled her nose, a happy feeling.

They had finished their house and moved in just two days before. What an exciting time it had been. There were actually two separate log structures, both under a single roof. A wide breezeway—called a dogtrot—separated them. Both buildings were wide and long, divided into separate rooms. One side contained a family room and kitchen. A high rock fireplace dominated the large family room. Across the breezeway, the other building contained three bedrooms, one of which was Julianna's. It was her very first room of her own.

Moving into their new home brought a new brightness to her mother's face. The discouraged, downtrodden look had disappeared. Julianna even caught her mother and father exchanging loving glances lately, the first time in a long time. Even the twins were easier to get along with.

The sweet aroma of fresh coffee wafted in and motivated Julianna to climb from her soft feather bed. She padded barefoot to the single window and gazed out. The early morning sun splayed across Angle Fire Mountain and set it ablaze with a panorama of fall color: Deep reds, shades of orange and yellow, and the shimmering gold of the Aspen groves created a picture no living artist could duplicate. The sun's rays bounced off a misty fog that hovered above the falls and crowned it with a colorful rainbow.

The sight took her breath away. This has got to be the most beautiful valley in the entire world, she thought.

Reluctantly, she tore herself from the breathtaking sight, quickly washed and dressed, and hurried to join the family for breakfast. She was late. Her mother was just taking the biscuits from the Dutch oven as she rushed in.

"I'm sorry, mother," she apologized. "It was such a wonderful morning, I overslept."

"I know dear. Your father and I slept in, also. The boys still aren't up. Everyone has worked so hard getting the house finished, I think we all deserved a little rest."

"I couldn't agree more," her father said. "But there's chores to be done. Julianna, go get your brothers up. They'd stay in bed all day if we'd let them. Those poor cows are bawling their heads off to be milked and fed."

Julianna hurried out the door and across the breezeway to the twin's bedroom. She tapped on the door. Hearing no answer she pushed the door open. Just as she knew they would be, her brothers were sprawled out on the big feather bed, arms and legs askew.

Plucking a feather protruding from the bed, she leaned over and tickled Dewey's lip and nose. He sleepily swiped an arm across his mouth and wiggled his lips. She repeated the prank. Lifting a hand, he scratched his lip, then opened his eyes. Seeing her and realizing what was happening, he bolted from the bed with a feather pillow and lit out after her. Using her hands to ward off the swinging pillow, she backed up, laughing all the while.

"Pa says to get up and eat breakfast," she told him as she retreated. "He says there's chores to do and you're late. You better hurry, he's awfully mad."

"They're coming," she told her father as she swung back into the family room and poured him another cup of coffee.

She sprinkled flour in the big black skillet to make gravy while her mother turned the frying potatoes in another pan. The smell of breakfast cooking, the sound of laughter, the feeling of family, all these washed over her, flooding her with emotions that made her skin tingle.

"Isn't this the most beautiful place you've ever seen?" She asked.

"It certainly is," her mother agreed. "I never dreamed we could find a place like this. We never would have if it hadn't been for Jedidiah."

The mere mention of his name tugged memories from the recesses of her mind. She closed her eyes and relived the memory of their kiss for the thousandth time. She could still feel his gentle touch on her cheek...the depth of his stare into her eyes, as if he could look right into her very soul. She remembered the caress of his lips on hers...so tender...yet so strong. As it did each time, the memory sent shivers of excitement surging through her body. Her thoughts were scattered by her father's voice.

"I don't know what we would have done without Mose and Minnie's help," her father was saying. "One thing for shore, we wouldn't be in our house by now without them. I reckon that big fellow can do mite-near anything. I told them not to bother coming down off the mountain today, seeing as how we've got most everything finished."

The twins hurried in and took their place on the bench on one side of the long, plank table. Julianna took her place on the other side. Mr. Johnson sat at one end and Mrs. Johnson at the other. Like they always did at mealtime, they joined hands around the table.

"Let's thank the Lord for His bounty," Wesley Johnson said as everyone bowed their heads.

"Now, Lord. We don't rightly know why you've, all of a sudden, been so good to us. We ain't complaining, mind you. Goodness knows we've seen more'n our share of hard times, but even then, we know you didn't forget about us. We thank you for our new home...and, Lord...watch out after our friend, Jedidiah, too. Amen."

"Pa," Dewey mumbled around a mouthful of biscuit and sorghum molasses. "After we get the chores done, you reckon me and Denver could go fishing down in the river? We saw some fish in there yesterday as long as my arm."

"Don't talk with your mouth full." Their mother scolded.

"I don't see why not," their father replied. "After you get your chores done, mind you."

"Yes, sir."

"Boys," their mother said. "After you get through milking, I want you to fill up the wash pot and both of the tubs with water from the spring. Julianna and I have a week's washing to do today."

"Awe, mom, the fish probably won't be biting by then. We was hoping to catch enough for supper."

"You heard your mother," Wesley Johnson told them firmly. "You do like she says and I don't want to hear no sassing, you hear?"

"Yes, sir," Dewey said.

After breakfast they all set in doing their chores. The twins grabbed a bucket and headed out to milk and feed Sadie. Mr. Johnson swiped his hat from the wall peg and clamped it on his head.

"Wesley, I sure would like it if you'd string us up a clothes line before you get too busy," Adrienne said.

"I'll go ahead and do that before I start chopping wood. We've got to start laying in wood for the winter. It'll be here before you know it. Mose says the snow starts flying by late November. We've got to get that barn done before then, too."

"Julianna," her mother said. "I'll clear the table and do the dishes if you'll make the beds and straighten up. I want us to keep our new house fit."

"Yes, mother."

Julianna turned to leave the room, then stopped and turned around.

"Mom, how old were you when you and pa got married?"

She watched a knowing smile crease her mother's lips. Her mother didn't answer for a long minute. She just stared at the stack of dirty dishes in her hands, her mind seemingly lost in memories of long ago.

"I was just almost two years younger than you," she finally answered. "I was only seventeen. Wesley and his father came to our farm to buy a wagonload of corn. I knew the minute I saw him, he was the one for me. He must have known it, too. That very day he asked my pa if he could come calling."

"Did pa kiss you on your first date?"

"Yes, as a matter of fact he did. He asked my pa if he could take me to a barn dance over in Poplar Bluff. I was surprised when pa let me go. He came and picked me up in their wagon. It was a wonderful dance. He kissed me on the way home."

"When did he ask you to marry him?"

"You sure are asking a lot of questions, young lady."

"How else am I supposed to find out about these things?

"It was about a month later," her mother explained. "We went to a pie supper at the Church in town. On the way home he stopped the wagon and...and asked me to marry him. The preacher married us the following Saturday."

For a long time Julianna just stood there thinking. Could she dare hope her and Jedidiah might...one day...share their lives as man and wife? Did she dare dream such an impossible dream? She decided she would weep less for dreams that might never come true, than if she refused to dream at all.

Jedidiah had slept little. Excitement at being so close to home denied the sleep his body so desperately needed. He had spent most of the night staring up into the endless ebony expanse that was blacker than the blackest black. Tiny pinpoints of light marked the home of a myriad of stars. Sometime before daylight he finally gave up and coiled from his bedroll.

He coaxed last night's campfire to life and set his blackened coffeepot over the flames. While it was coming to a boil, he saddled his pinto and set about loading the heavy packs on Mule, as well as the two extra packhorses he had bought in Sante Fe. The added supplies would help both him and the Johnsons make it through the winter without having to make a long trip into Taos.

Finishing his task, he strolled over to the little mountain stream and washed in the icy-cold water. Returning to the fire, he squatted on his haunches and poured steaming coffee into a tin cup. Blowing the steam away, he tested the hot liquid. It was thick and bitter, but went down good on the frosty morning.

His thoughts wandered back to the meeting with Mr. Fargo and Winston before leaving Sante Fe. The Wells Fargo President had been overly generous with both his praise and his money. Jedidiah's eyes instinctively flicked to the saddlebags tied behind his saddle. They contained two hundred fifty shiny new gold double-eagles—twelve thousand dollars, two thousand more than he had originally been promised—for the safe return of the girls.

"We'll call it a bonus for a job well done," Fargo had said.

Dog trotted up and nuzzled his leg, as if expecting the pat Jedidiah always gave him.

"It won't be long now, big fellow," he spoke to his companion, ruffling the hair around the dog's neck. "We'll be home today for shore."

He figured with any luck, he ought to make the valley by mid-afternoon. It sure will be good to get back home, he mused. Wonder if Julianna and her family made it to the valley okay? Reckon they've got their cabin done yet?

The thought of Julianna brought with it a flush of excitement. He remembered their parting kiss: The softness of her lips, the way she had returned his kiss; the little moan that came from her throat. Lord-almighty she had tasted good!

He had played, and replayed it over and over on the long ride from Sante Fe. He had made up his mind. If she would have him, he intended to ask Julianna to marry him. She could easily have any man, any man at all, though he figured that she—shy, modest, and oblivious of her sensual allure—would not think so. Still, if indeed she would agree to be his wife, as long as he lived, he never wanted her to regret that choice.

Most of his life he had lived out of his saddlebags, always itching to discover what was over the next mountain. He reckoned as how that came from his Boone heritage. That was all behind him now; he was ready to settle down, to raise a family—strong sons to carry on the family name.

Anticipation got the better of him. He tossed the remainder of his coffee on the fire, rinsed the pot in the stream, and stomped the fire out, sending a cloud of cherry-red sparks drifting skyward.

"Let's hit the trail, Dog," he said, pushing to his feet. "We still got a piece to go."

The sun had heeled over to the west and started its downward journey toward the horizon.

Julianna and her mother had spent the whole day doing the washing. Denver was chopping wood and stacking it in a long pile inside the breezeway. Her father was up on top of the new barn, nailing down wooden shingles Dewey tossed up to him.

Julianna used the poke stick to fish the last of her father's work clothes from the bubbling water in the black wash pot. Using the stick, she transported them to the soapy washtub that sat on the new wash bench Mose had built.

Sloshing the heavy work pants around, she began the laborious process of scrubbing them. The strong lye soap burned her hands and, like always, she scraped her knuckles on the rough scrub board. Over and over she applied the big square bar of soap, then rubbed the clothes until they were clean. She wrung them out, then sloshed them into the second tub that contained rinse water. Piece by piece she removed them, wrung them out, and tossed them into the large wicker basket.

Finally, when the last article lay twisted in the basket, now brimming with sodden laundry, she bent and struggled awkwardly to heft it to one hip. Carrying the basket, she headed for the long rope clothesline her father had strung just that morning.

Folding the wet clothes over the line, she uttered a small prayer of thankfulness that the weekly washday was almost over. As she lifted the last article and doubled it across the line, something inside her caused her eyes to lift.

A lone rider, leading three heavy laden pack mules, emerged from the forest at the far side of the valley. Her eyes narrowed...and a hand lifted to shield them from the sun. Suddenly she gasped on a quick intake of air. Her heart leaped. Even at a distance of more than a mile, she recognized Jedidiah's pinto.

"Mama! Papa!" she screamed. "It's Jedidiah! He's home!"

Julianna broke into a run. Her feet flew across the grassy valley floor. Her heart raced even faster than her feet. Her breath came in short, labored gasps. He's home! She told herself as she ran to meet him. He's home safe.

Jedidiah saw the cabin the minute he broke out of the trees. They had chosen the location well. Using the tall pines as a backdrop, they had built their home in the edge of a clearing close to one of the many springs that dotted the valley. It was a large, sturdy looking house of peeled logs with a breezeway tunneling through the center. Two giant oak trees shaded the front. A long tendril of smoke wafted from the tall, fieldstone chimney surmounting the roof and billowed up, only to swirl away, ghostlike on a northerly wind. It sure looked like a homey place.

His quick, sweeping gaze showed Mr. Johnson working on the roof of a new barn. One of the twins was helping from below. Another was chopping wood, the sound of his ax echoed across the valley. Julianna stood at a clothesline, hanging clothes across it. He heard her cry of recognition and watched as she ran to meet him.

It was a sight to behold...long dress hiked up to free her feet for running, she flew across the valley toward him like a young doe, fleet and lithe. Her long hair, lifted by the breeze and filtered by the afternoon sun, billowed behind her like strands of spun gold.

A great surge of emotion, steeped in both pride and humility, swept over him like a river over sand, eroding the self-confidence he had felt before. The little speech he had practiced a thousand times on the trip from Sante Fe suddenly dissolved like a puff of smoke in the wind. She is the most beautiful woman in the whole world. How could I even think she would marry a saddle tramp like me?

Nevertheless, he summoned up the last bit of his dwindling courage and dropped the lead ropes to his pack mules. He caught a glimpse of Mr. Johnson standing on top of the barn. He saw the man swipe off his hat and begin waving it in the air. Jedidiah kicked the pinto into a gallop.

The distance between them closed quickly. Reining Butternut to a skidding stop, Jedidiah leaped from the saddle and hit the ground running. He ran to meet her. His outstretched arms reached toward her as her arms did to him. He saw a smile stretch her lips and glimpsed happy tears breach her eyes as she plunged into his open arms. Arms grasped in a hungry embrace...and, for a long minute, they held each other.

"Oh Jedidiah," she sobbed happily into his chest. "I've missed you so much. I'm so happy you're home safe."

With a soft hand he raised her face...their gazes locked...He stared deep into those misty-green eyes. I could drown in the green, shimmering depths of those eyes, he thought.

"Julianna," he whispered, wanting to hear the name on his tongue. "You're so beautiful."

His knuckles glided slowly, tantalizingly, across her cheek, brushing the tears away, savoring the softness, feeling the thrill of the touch radiate up his arm and race straight to his heart.

Julianna's eyes closed. From her parted lips came a soft gasp. Her eyelids fluttered open again and allowed him entry into her heart through her eyes. They welcomed him...absorbed him...drew him deeper and deeper into her very soul. Is this really happening? Julianna asked herself. Is he really here? Or is this just another of my dreams?

Her senses scattered and were carried away by the wind. Her head spun deliriously. Her body flushed with a fevered fanaticism. A surge of tiny tremors shook her, and then another, starting deep at her core and pulsing through her body like ripples across the top of calm water.

A low moan emanated from her throat as their open lips raced to meet each other, clashing like starving creatures...testing...tasting...devouring each other...locked in the age-old ritual of love. Time was caught and held suspended for a long slice of eternity.

Her clutching hands crept up his neck. Slender fingers splayed, burrowing in his long, corn silk hair, drawing him tighter to her. Her heart beat against Jedidiah's own. Her head spun. She felt as though her very bones dissolved within her. Her knees shook so that, somehow, she knew she would collapse were he not holding her so tightly.

"I love you, Julianne," he gasped against her lips. "Will you marry me?"

"Oh, yes, darling, yes. Yes. Oh Yes!" Dreams really can come true, she thought.

~The End~

About the Author

I was born and raised in eastern Oklahoma—formerly known as the Indian Territory. My home was only a half-day's ride by horseback from old historic Fort Smith, Arkansas, home of Judge Isaac C. Parker, who became famous as "The Hanging Judge."

As a young boy I rode the same trails once ridden by the likes of the James, Younger, and Dalton gangs. The infamous "Bandit Queen", Belle Starr's home and grave were only thirty miles from my own home. I grew up listening to stories of lawmen and outlaws.

For as long as I can remember I love to read, and the more I read the more I wanted to write. Hundreds of poems, songs, and short stories only partially satisfied my love of writing. Dozens of stories of the "old west" gathered dust on the shelves of my mind. When I retired I began to take down those stories, dust them off, and do what I had dreamed of doing ever since I was a small boy—writing historical western novels.